Conan

the

Dandelion

⚓ *I.J Hidee* ⚓

Conan the Dandelion

Paperback edition published in 2021.

Author I.J Hidee

Edition and correction 2021 © I.J Hidee

Also by I.J Hidee

The Class Prince
The Prick and His Prince
Y.O.L.O
Conan the Dandelion
Darker Parker
The Ranking System #1
The Rankless System #2
The Fall of the System #3

For those who feel misunderstood by the

world

Table of Contents

Prologue

Dear,

By the time you read this, I will already be gone. But before I leave, I wanted to write you this letter. I'm not sure whether it is crueler to leave with or without a goodbye, but farewells have never been joyous. I don't know if you'll find this note or if you'll read it, but I hope you do.

Firstly, I want you to know that no matter what happens, know that it isn't your fault. I've realized throughout my life that people blame themselves for things that aren't their fault. It's a strange mechanism us humans have, one that I'm familiar with. So if you read this, please know that you've done nothing wrong.

Secondly, I'd like to thank you. Before coming to the Big City, my life felt like a dark hole and a constant struggle. But after I met you, Freddie, Zev, and all the beautiful people of this world, I was able to experience true happiness. Words will never express how thankful I am to have met you. I will forever be grateful to the world for connecting our lives and intertwining our fates. I have many regrets, but you will never be one of them.

I don't know if I've mustered up the courage to tell you this—I hope I did—but know that I love you. They may be trivial words to you, perhaps they won't mean anything, but I have, and always will love you.

Yours truly

Chapter 1: A Temporary Home

Graduation wasn't like in the movies.

The ceremony was nowhere near as perfect or glorious as they portrayed it on screen. The cap-throwing tradition wasn't as fun as we'd hoped. We took them off and threw them high into the air, only for them to swoop back down like a flock of angry crows. The caps hit many of us in the face, some in the eye. Who knew graduation could be so dangerous?

Students and families were crying, but their tears weren't dribbling off their chins like metaphorical raindrops. No, they were ugly crying. Snot and mucus trailed down their faces as they rubbed their bloodshot eyes. Girls had mascara streaks stretch down their faces, which only worsened when they tried to rub it away. They stopped crying whenever someone came up to them asking for pictures. They'd quickly dab away their tears and put on a smile, and I thought it was impressive and sad how people forced themselves to smile even though they were sad. After the photos, they'd continue crying as if it were the end of the world. Perhaps to some people, it was. High school was over, and we would become "real adults," as our teachers would say. I didn't know what they meant. Did that mean some adults were fake? How does one fake being an adult?

I wasn't happy or sad that day, but even if I didn't have any friends in high school, I knew I'd miss many people, like the cafeteria lady who had a hairy mole on her chin. I think I'll miss her the most. She was always nice to me and made Russian jokes that I never understood. I assumed they were jokes because she would start laughing hysterically by herself, so I'd laugh along with her. I'm going to miss her snort-laughs.

After graduation, my parents gave me some money to take a gap year. Ever since my early teens, they'd treated me differently. Even though they'd never said it aloud, I knew it was because of the Incident. We never talked about the Incident, but that didn't mean it didn't happen. My parents felt guilty—people often blamed themselves for their loved ones—but it wasn't their fault. During my gap year, I went to Europe. Something about seeing unknown places and meeting new people altered you. It reminded you that the world held so much diversity and that one could never discover all the world's mysteries in the span of a lifetime. After traveling alone, I applied to a university far away from home, wanting to move to a bigger city. My family seemed particularly nervous when I left.

The thought of going somewhere populated by so many people terrified me, but it also reassured me. My hometown was so small that everyone knew each other. But in a big city, where important people had important things to do, it was easy to blend in and become part of the crowd. The possibility of being anonymous intrigued me. Some people wanted to become famous, others wanted to be rich—I wanted to be a nobody.

Though, even if I couldn't be a somebody to the world, I'd like to be a somebody to someone. I would like to make a friend in the Big City. My doctors and therapists told me it would help me get better, but rather than trying to cure myself, I wanted to experience friendship before the End. I gave myself exactly ten months to experience happiness. Perhaps I was being too ambitious, but it was good to set goals. They gave you a reason to keep going. Ten months, I told myself, and then I'd leave the Big City.

I drove for five hours before arriving at my new apartment. It was near my university and was relatively cheap, so I chose it. I parked my car beside a jet-black motorcycle, opened the trunk, and took out my luggage. I didn't bring much with me. A short, stubby man with salt and pepper hair stood in front of the old building. He squinted his eyes as if he was looking for something. I think he was looking for me.

"You must be Conan!" he exclaimed, jogging down the stairs and joining me. He must be the landlord. The man gave out his hand, but I offered him a small wave.

"Hello." I smiled. "My name is Conan."

He blinked, then slowly lowered his hand. "I'm Greg, the one you exchanged e-mails with these past few weeks. I'm here to give you a quick apartment tour."

I smiled. "That's very nice of you."

He chuckled, scratching his beard. "It's kind of my job."

I blinked, not knowing what to say. "That's very nice of you," I repeated with a smile.

He blinked, stared, and masked his confusion with a stiff smile. "Sure," he replied with a nod. "Is that your car over there?"

"Yes, that's mine."

"You can park there today, but you might want to park elsewhere tomorrow."

"Why?"

"The owner gets protective over his motorcycle and likes to keep two empty spaces on each side to avoid potential scratches. He's a spoiled brat if you ask me, and he's arrogant too. I guess it's not surprising considering that he's the son of a rich doctor. Anyway, here, lemme help you with your bags."

"It's okay, I can carry them."

"You're so small, I'm scared you might break your back."

Before I could protest, Greg picked up my bags and walked into the building. I followed him, admiring the dirty walls that peeled. There was a strange smell too, as if someone had died here. I stopped in my steps with wide eyes. A chalk outline formed the shape of a body on the floor.

"Greg, did someone die here?" I asked.

Greg looked at the yellow tape and let out a nervous chuckle. "Oh, that? That's just a decoration we did for Halloween. We forgot to remove it, but don't worry, we'll remove it ASAP," he assured, stepping over the outline. Before I could ask any more questions, he spoke first. "This is a small residence. There are five floors, and you live on the fourth."

He carried the luggage up the creaky stairs.

"Wouldn't it be easier to take the elevator?" I asked.

13

"The elevator is broken, but we'll get that repaired ASAP, no worries. You don't mind using the stairs for a few days, do you?"

"No, it's okay. I enjoy walking."

"Your luggage isn't as heavy as I thought it'd be. Is this all you brought with you?"

"I'm not staying for very long," I said with a small smile.

We went to the fourth floor, and Greg opened the door with a rusty key, which he handed me. He gave me a tour of my new home, but it was so small that you could see everything without moving.

"Oh, and we're having some problems with the pipes," Greg said when he showed me the bathroom. "You might not have hot water for a couple of days, but we'll get that fixed ASAP."

I nodded. I think Greg was used to reassuring newcomers because his voice took a mechanical tone, as if he had memorized his words by script.

"If you need any help, you have my number."

I nodded and thanked him. "Goodbye, Greg," I replied, waving at him.

His hairy eyebrows pulled together. "Uh, yes, goodbye, Conan." He gave me one last glance before leaving.

I began unpacking my things and cleaned the house. I brought some clothes, shoes, and my journals. I carefully hid the notebooks under my clothes in my drawer, except for the most recent one, which I placed under my pillow. I always wrote before going to bed. When I was done, I took a shower and yelped when the cold water poured over my head. Greg was right, the pipes were broken, and there was no hot water. I felt like I was hyperventilating, gasping, and yelping as I tried to wash my hair and body as quickly as I could. I wore a fresh pair of clothes, but I could still feel goosebumps layering my skin. I headed to my room to find warmer clothes, but the doorbell rang, followed by an impatient knock.

Did Greg forget something?

I unlocked the door and opened it, surprised to see not Greg but a tall boy with tousled black hair and piercing eyes. His body loomed over mine, casting a shadow that made day seem like night, and his chiseled jaw tightened.

Whoever he was, he didn't seem happy.

Chapter 2: My First Friend

I gaped at him curiously, admiring his sharp jaw, chin, and high cheekbones. His eyes were midnight black, and he ran a hand through his tousled, dark hair. I caught a glimpse of his thick brows. Oh, and he had a nice forehead. He studied me in return, his eyes looking up and down my body. The lean muscles in his forearms bulged when he crossed his arms over his strong chest. He was scowling, but I thought he'd look more handsome if he smiled.

I realized we had been staring at each other for a while and wondered if this was awkward for him.

"Hello," I said, greeting him with a smile and wave. "My name is Conan."

"Where is the old fucker?" His voice was husky and harsh.

I blinked. The books I'd read told me that if you introduced yourself, the other person would reply in the same manner. I believe that is what society called etiquette. My notes have never prepared me for an answer like his. So I tried again.

"Hello, my name is Conan."

"That's great. Now, where is Greg?"

"I don't know. Where is he?"

I wasn't trying to make a joke. I genuinely didn't know where Greg went. The tall boy must have thought that I was mocking him. He narrowed his eyes into slits. Then he noticed my half-dried hair.

"You took a shower?"

I patted my head. "Yes."

"Hot water runs in your place?" he asked, anger returning in his charcoal eyes. Before I could answer, he walked past me and headed to the bathroom.

I wanted to stop him, but then I remembered he had a strong chest and rigid arms. I was built like a bean sprout. The wind could knock me down. Perhaps it was best if I avoided engaging in a physical conflict with this man. I heard him turn on the shower, and a loud yelp and a string of curse words followed. Seconds later, he stormed out with water dripping from the tip of his fingers.

"You lied. The water is cold."

I frowned. "I never said it wasn't."

"You said you took a shower."

"A cold shower," I clarified.

"You took a *cold* shower? What's wrong with you?"

"A lot of things, I think. But the doctors say I'm getting better."

He paused, looked at me, then furrowed his eyebrows, as if he realized something crucial.

"Wait, who are you again?"

"My name is Conan. I just moved in. What's your name?"

"Gloria moved out?"

"That's a very unique name!"

He looked like he wanted to punch me.

"So you have the keys to this place and everything?"

I nodded.

"Was Greg the one who gave you the keys?"

"Yes, but he left about fifteen minutes ago. Greg is a very nice man."

"Greg is a *liar*," he muttered, taking out a pack of cigarettes from his shirt pocket. He brought it to his lips and lit the tip. His movement was quick and swift, showing years of expertise. I didn't know we were allowed to smoke in the building.

"Did Greg tell you he'd get the broken elevator fixed?" he asked, letting out a puff of smoke.

I nodded, admiring his beautiful hands. They were long and slim, almost feminine, contrasting with the rest of his body.

"Did he also tell you he would fix the pipes?"

I nodded again.

"And did he tell you that the chalk outlining a body downstairs was a Halloween decoration?" He snorted.

"He did."

"He says that to all the newcomers. The hot water won't be running any time soon, and expect to walk up and down those musty stairs for as long as you live here. Oh, and you're an idiot if you believe that the tape downstairs is decoration."

I blinked. "I'm an idiot?"

"Seems so." He shrugged, the cigarettes hanging from his lips. He leaned his shoulder against the wall, his eyes locked on the burning tip as he inhaled. His gaze was so intimidating you'd think that his eyes were why the fire burned.

He looked as if he was deep in thought during those few quick seconds, and I wondered what he thought about as he filled his lungs with smoke. Something about him was captivating.

"How long do you plan on living here?" he asked.

"Not very long," I answered.

"Good. The quicker you leave, the better. As for Greg, I wouldn't trust a word he says."

"What about you? Can I trust you?"

He paused. Then, a crooked smile curved on his lips.

"Not if you're smart."

"But you said I was an idiot."

He gave me a simple shrug with a grin unlike any other.

"I'm Parker, your upstairs neighbor."

He pointed up, and I raised my gaze. The paint on the ceiling was starting to peel.

"Conan, right?" he said.

I nodded, happy he remembered. A warm feeling spread through me whenever someone said my name. Sometimes, I'd wonder if my life was an imagination or if I was a ghost recounting his past, but then someone would say my name, reminding me that I truly existed.

"That's me," I said with a smile.

"Welcome to the crappiest building of this city."

"Thank you."

"How old are you? You don't look old enough to live on your own."

"I'm twenty-one years old."

His eyebrows shot up in surprise.

"What about you?"

"Guess," he said with a playful smirk.

"Thirty?"

Parker choked on his saliva. His dark eyes pierced through me. "I'm not an old man. I'm younger than you."

He placed his cigarette between his lips.

"I'm twenty," he finally declared.

Despite the scowl on his face, Parker seemed very sociable. I liked how straightforward he was. There weren't many people like him. I was grateful that he was leading the conversation because I never really knew what to say to strangers, but Parker kept the conversation going as if it was second nature.

"So, you're a college student?" he asked, finishing his cigarette.

I nodded. "I applied to Bergson University."

"I guess we'll be seeing each other often. What do you major in?"

"Philosophy."

He snorted. "Philosophy? Who majors in philosophy?"

"Me."

He rolled his eyes. "It was a rhetorical question."

"Oh. Are you an English major?"

Parker looked even more exhausted than when he first walked in. Another thing I noticed about him was the dark circles under his eyes. But he was so good-looking that you were too busy admiring everything else. Like his forehead.

"I major in bio-chem," he said dismissively.

"Do you like bio-chem?"

"Absolutely hate it, but I'm good at it."

I frowned. "Why do you study something you hate?"

"Didn't you hear the last part?"

"That you're good at it?" I asked.

"Exactly. And it'll get me a decent job that pays well, and that's all that matters."

"I don't think that's all that matters."

He raised his shoulders. "It is what it is."

Parker walked past me, which I guess was a sign that he was leaving. I watched him head for the door, and although I was sad to see him leave, I waved at him.

"Why do you keep doing that?"

"Doing what?"

"Smiling and waving like the penguins from Madagascar."

"I read it in a book," I replied.

"Read what in a book?"

"That smiling and waving help you make friends."

Parker gave me *The Look*.

"You're weird, you know that?" He didn't say it in a mocking tone. It sounded more like he was stating a bio-chem fact.

"I'm sorry."

"Don't apologize," he said harshly.

I looked for something else to say, and all I could think of was, "Okay."

"And stop waving, it's already been a couple of seconds."

"I'm waiting for you to wave back."

He stared at me as if I was an alien from outer space, ran a hand through his tousled hair, then headed for the door. He dismissively waved his hand over his shoulder without looking back.

"See you around, Dandelion."

Dandelion? My name is Conan.

"Bye, Parker!" I exclaimed, watching him disappear up the staircase.

I smiled widely.

I think I made my first friend.

Chapter 3: Philip George

A week had passed since I moved into my new apartment. I bought flowers and plants to decorate the house but left the walls empty and plain. My clothes and underwear were neatly folded in the closet and drawers, and all my books were stacked on the shelf. Nothing else in this house belonged to me. Well, there was me. I guess I belonged to myself. Anyway, I digress.

I pulled out a notebook that Dr. Philip gave me. The task he had given me before I left my hometown was to write one new dish every week. I called it the "*Recipe Book Never Use,*" but Dr. Philip told me it wasn't catchy enough, which was his nice way of telling me he disapproved of the title. So he re-baptized it as "*Conan's Recipe Book.*" But it wasn't my recipe book because the recipes weren't mine. I found them online. But I didn't want to upset Dr. Philip, so only when I was alone did I call it "*The Recipe Book I Never Use,*" but that's between you and me.

I flipped through the pages and stopped at the turkey sandwich recipe. I followed the instructions one by one: two slices of bread, a slice of turkey, mayonnaise, shreds of lettuce, and cheese. I carefully stacked the ingredients and cut the sandwich into triangles. I sat at the table and smiled, happy with the result. But that was it. I was pleased with the result but had no desire to eat the finished product. I picked up the sandwich nonetheless.

"I will eat," I said aloud.

I took a bite and chewed. I took another, then another, and then stopped at my fourth when I realized I was chewing but hadn't swallowed. I put the sandwich down because I couldn't take another bite.

My stomach had already burned, and my chest twisted. Or perhaps it was my stomach that twisted and my chest that burned. I wasn't good at expressing my pain, I just knew that eating felt wrong. Eating meant living. I stared at the plate, hoping I'd develop an appetite. I stared at the sandwich, wishing it would miraculously disappear.

I gave up.

"Next time," I whispered to myself. I didn't want to waste the food, so I shielded it with plastic wrap and put it in the fridge. I felt relieved when I left the kitchen, as if a heavy burden had been removed from my shoulders.

I washed up in the same cold water I had been showering in for the past few days. Though, some part of me enjoyed the stinging water that pricked my skin. When I finished, I scurried to my eternal safe place: my bedroom. I crawled onto my bed and turned off the lights, snuggling under the sheets. I counted my fingers and then wiggled my toes to make sure all of them were there.

I closed my eyes and tried to sleep, but my phone buzzed. There was only one person who would call me at this hour. He was the only person who would call me at all.

"Good evening, Dr. Philip," I answered.

"Good evening, Conan."

His calm voice made me nervous.

"How are you?" he asked.

I stared at the ceiling. I couldn't see in the dark, but I knew I was staring at the ceiling.

"Good." I paused. "I think."

"That's good, that's great. Good is good. Good is great," he said, his voice superficially upbeat. I could hear him writing something down. Doctors like him were told to be optimistic with their patients. Apparently, it helped the healing process, so they'd often use words like good, fantastic, and sometimes *spectacular*. I didn't quite understand what they meant by "Healing Process." I didn't have any physical wounds. Perhaps it was a metaphor. Or perhaps they were trying to repair something invisible. But if the wounds weren't visible, did they really exist? Again, I digress.

"Have you taken your medicine?"

"Yes."

"Have you been eating three meals a day?"

"I'm trying."

I could hear more scribbles and felt somewhat discouraged.

"What about sleep?"

"I'm trying as well."

"Have you contacted your family yet? Told your friends about your new life in the Big City? That's quite a big change for you. Why did you decide to move away?"

There were too many questions, and I had a hard time keeping up.

"Yes. No. Yes. I don't know."

"Have you found a local doctor in the city?"

I had to change doctors since Dr. Philip's clinic was four hours away from where I was. He told me he'd check up on me now and then but that I'd have to find another doctor nearby.

"I've been a little busy."

"With?" He sounded both disappointed and enthusiastic.

"Reading books. And writing. Lots of writing."

"Oh, that kind of busy," his voice fell into flat disappointment. "Well, I'm glad you're being productive, but try to go out more, okay? Get some fresh air and make new friends. Oh, and find a clinic soon. We need to check up on your health."

"I'm doing better," I murmured.

"Yes, I know, but you still need a doctor."

"You don't trust me?"

"It's not that I don't trust you. It's just that I want to make sure you're healthy. We care about you. Okay?"

Who was *we*?

"Okay."

"Promise me you'll look for a doctor?"

"I can't make promises, but I'll try," I said. And I would. I just didn't know if I'd succeed. I probably wouldn't, but that was what I liked about trying. Nothing was certain.

"I believe in you, Conan, okay?"

I wiggled my toes. "Okay."

"Contact your family or me if there's anything wrong. Okay?"

"Okay."

"Are you getting ready to sleep now?"

"Yes." I wasn't great at keeping up conversations or asking questions, but Dr. Philip was a professional. Although, I much preferred talking with Parker. His questions were more genuine, and I felt more comfortable with him, even though we'd only met once. Dr. Philip's questions were more like a list of sentences he asked his patients to ensure they were still intact.

"Conan?" said Dr. Philip.

I snapped out of thoughts and realized that I had missed his question. "I'm sorry, I wasn't listening."

"Have the Dark Thoughts been coming back?"

I stiffened. "No, not since I moved in."

"That's good. Maybe moving to the city was a good idea after all. It's a nice place to be in. Lots of people, diverse activities..." he listed the perks of living in the Big City. I wondered how he knew this place so well, despite never having lived here. I found it strange that people talked about things they'd never experienced themselves.

"Do you have anything you want to do there?"

I smiled. "I'd like to ride the city bus."

"The city bus?" he echoed.

"Yes, the public transportation that takes individuals to their desired destination," I clarified, just in case.

"Yes, of course, the bus." There was a pause. "Is there anything else you'd like to do? Something you look forward to?"

I'd like to meet my upstairs neighbor again. He had a nice forehead.

"No, I can't think of anything right now."

"I'm sure you'll think of something. There are so many things you can do in life, Conan. So many," he murmured.

I didn't know what else to say. "Okay," was the best I could think of.

"Find a doctor soon and keep me updated on how you're doing."

"Okay."

"Goodnight, Conan."

That was the social cue to hang up.

"Goodnight, Philip George." I paused. "May I call you Philip George?"

Dr. Philip's full name was Philip George. I saw it once on a file when I was in his office.

"Yes, Conan, you can call me Philip George." He sounded tired.

I smiled. "Thank you, Philip George. Goodnight, Philip George."

Even though we were on the phone, I had the strange sense that he was giving me *The Look*. He hung up, and I tucked my phone under my pillow. What a nice man.

Chapter 4: Freddie the Troll

A loud banging noise woke me up in the middle of the night. During my first night in my new apartment, I learned why Parker had dark circles under his eyes. Instead of sleeping, he spent his hours doing other activities.

The walls were so thin that I could hear everything that was going on upstairs. I could hear his voice and a woman's voice. Sometimes there were multiple female voices, but Parker's was always there. The noises comprised creaking, banging, moaning, screaming, and other things I'd rather not mention. I read that humans should have at least seven hours of sleep to lead a good and healthy life. Parker had four at most.

I dug my head under my pillow, hoping to block the noise, but I could still hear him. Well, *them.*

This went on for the rest of the week. On Sunday, I went upstairs to ask Parker if he could make less noise. Tomorrow was my first day of college, and I didn't want to fall asleep during class. I climbed the creaky stairs, still wearing my pajamas and fluffy shark slippers. The fifth floor had a long corridor with one door on each side. I pressed my ear against the door on the right.

This was Parker's house.

I gently knocked against the hard surface, but he must not have heard. I tried again, this time a little louder. The noises stopped and were then followed by footsteps. The door clicked open. Parker was wearing nothing but black briefs that he was still adjusting around his waist. The elastic band gently slapped against his skin when he pulled his thumb away, but his prominent hip bones were still very visible. Parker was built with clean lines and lean muscles. He had abs and muscular thighs. He looked more like a man than someone who was twenty.

It was dark, and the only light source was the moon that shone through the windows. Parker was half shadow, every muscle in his torso flowing from the light into the dark. Every move gave away his strength.

He smelled like cigarettes, alcohol, cologne, and sex. Lots of it. Parker casually ran a hand through his hair, then wiped away the sweat on his forehead. He didn't look flustered or embarrassed by the situation.

"Good evening, Parker," I said, retreating a step. I didn't feel comfortable being so close to his nude body.

"What do you want?" he asked.

"I was wondering if everything was okay. It sounded like you were fighting with someone."

A mischievous smirk curved on his face. "I guess you can put it that way," he said, winking so quickly I almost didn't catch it.

"I hope no one got hurt," I replied, trying to wink back. He scowled at the poor attempt.

"It's a good kind of hurt."

"A good hurt?"

"A pleasurable one," he clarified while clarifying nothing.

"Oh."

I didn't know what to say anymore. I had imagined our conversation in my head and even practiced in the mirror, but my mind was completely blank.

"Do you need anything else?" he inquired, his voice low and raspy.

"Your pleasurable fighting is very loud, and I can't sleep," I told him.

Parker's dark lashes fluttered. He let out a small sigh.

"Right, I forgot how thin these walls are. Sorry 'bout that, dandelion. Do you have any earphones? Maybe you can listen to some music until I'm finished?"

"My name is Conan, and I don't have earphones."

He stared at me. "What?"

"I said my name is Conan, and I don't have—"

"I heard what you said," he interrupted me, which was when I remembered that "what?" could mean multiple things. There was "what?" as in "what do you mean?", then there was "what?" as in "could you repeat that?", and then there was Parker's "what?", the "are you crazy?" kind of what.

"Did your earphones break or...?"

"No, I've never owned a pair."

Parker gave me *The Look*. He seemed so shocked that I think he forgot that he was wearing nothing but his briefs. They looked too tight for him, only in the middle area.

"Why?" he asked.

"I like listening to music without earphones."

31

Parker stared at me as if I had just announced that I was pregnant. His eyebrows furrowed as he tried to understand.

"What about when you're outside? How do you listen to music then?" he asked, leaning against the door frame and looking at me as if he was genuinely concerned for my wellbeing.

"I don't listen to music when I'm outside. I like listening to what's around me, like the birds or the wind or the leaves that rustle in the trees. Though, I don't like the sound of cars."

Parker blinked.

"I feel less disconnected to the world when I'm outside listening to what's around me," I tried to explain.

"That's, uh, great. Super spiritual. Peace and love, all that hippy chakra stuff. Anyway, do you want me to lend you some earplugs?"

Before I could answer, the door across from him swung open.

"No, dumbass, he wants you to shut up," snapped his neighbor, wearing a pink robe. The corridor lights flickered on (it took a moment for them to activate), revealing bright orange hair and a grumpy face. The boy had freckles sprinkled over his pale face, and he had a cute button nose.

"Oh great, it's Freddie the Troll," Parker grumbled under his breath.

"Yes, bitch, it's me. Now keep it down. There are people in this building who are trying to sleep. Like me and—" Freddie glanced, waiting for me to fill in the blank.

I waved at him. "Good evening, my name is Conan."

"Exactly. Like Conan and me," Freddie completed, his brown eyes flickering back to Parker.

"There are more important things than sleeping," Parker growled.

"Like what?"

"Like sexual pleasure."

Freddie scoffed. "Do they teach that in bio-chem?"

"Yes, as a matter of fact, they do. Don't be jealous just 'cause you can't get any."

"Get any what?" I asked curiously.

"Hush, Conan, the adults are talking," Parker snapped, his eyes still locked on Freddie.

"Oh, okay."

Parker and Freddie continued to bicker, and I couldn't tell if they were good friends or absolute enemies. The hallway lights turned off, so I hopped three times, and they turned back on.

"Jesus, Parker, are you drunk?" Freddie asked, squinting his eyes. I turned towards him and noticed how dilated Parker's pupils were.

Parker shrugged lazily. "A couple of shots."

"You said you'd stop drinking." Freddie sounded upset.

"I say a lot of dumb shit."

"I guess you're back to smoking too?"

"Get off my back, Fred. Not everyone is a stuck-up loser like you."

I frowned. "That's not very nice."

"Shut up, Conan."

"Hey, don't talk to Conan like that," Freddie snapped.

"Parker, where are you?" we heard a girl shout from inside his apartment.

"He's at the door. He'll be with you in a minute!" I replied.

Parker and Freddie's stared at me. Did I say something wrong? Freddie then turned his attention towards Parker.

"We don't need to hear your *amazing* sex life at 4 a.m. You can numb your misery with empty sex, alcohol, and cigarette, but at least do it quietly."

Maybe it was my lack of sleep, but I thought I saw a trace of pain register on Parker's face for a second. The hallway lights turned off, but when I jumped, and the lights flickered on, Parker's face returned to its usual scowl.

Freddie slammed the door so hard that the walls shook.

"Damn redhead," Parker grumbled.

"You mean Freddie?" I asked.

He narrowed his eyes at me. "*You're* still here?"

I patted my body to make sure I was. "Yes, I'm—"

"It was a rhetorical question. Gosh, what's wrong with you?!" he barked, slamming the door so hard behind him that I jumped.

I think he did it to annoy Freddie. I felt like I needed to slam a door to join in on their game, but there weren't any open doors for me to close.

I turned towards Freddie's door. "Goodnight, Freddie." And then I turned towards Parker's door. "Goodnight, Parker."

I headed downstairs, climbed into bed, pulled the sheets over my chest, and wriggled my toes. I thought I'd have to pull my pillow over my ears again, but to my surprise, the noises and creaking from above stopped. Despite his annoyance, Parker didn't wake us up for the rest of the night.

Chapter 5: The First Day

I had a good night's sleep thanks to Parker and Freddie. I climbed out of bed and prepared for my first day of college. I took a cold shower, brushed my teeth, and slipped into a fresh pair of clothes I had ironed the day before. Then came the hard part: breakfast. I made toast and eggs and sat at the table when everything was plated. I tried my best not to skip meals, especially breakfast, because apparently, it was the most important meal of the day, but it was also when I was the least hungry.

"You must eat healthy nutrients early in the morning to fuel your body." I could hear Dr. Philip George's voice echo in my mind. It took me a few minutes before taking a bite. I took another. And then another. And then stopped when my stomach told me no more.

"Next time," I murmured to myself, excited to get out of the kitchen and start the day. When I left the building, I saw Parker saddled over the big, black motorcycle I parked next to. The steel glistened under the bright sun, making me squint from the brightness. A girl was sitting behind him, wearing ripped black jeans and a bright red tank top that matched her bold lipstick. I watched as Parker adjusted a helmet on her head and assumed she was the girl he was pleasure fighting with. She was beautiful and looked like a model on a magazine cover. Both of them did.

Parker put on his black helmet, and the girl leaned forward, wrapping her slim arms around his waist. But the sudden image of Parker's strong, sweaty body and his prominent hips from last night flashed through my mind, and my throat tightened.

The motorcycle roared to life, and I watched as they zoomed out of the parking lot, disappearing down the road in the blink of an eye. It was the same scene in movies where a handsome young man drove away with a gorgeous woman on a motorcycle and disappeared into the sunset towards yonder. Except Parker was probably heading to university for his bio-chem class, a subject he hated studying.

"Don't mind him, Parker loves making dramatic exits," said a voice. I was so focused on Parker that I didn't notice Freddie walk out of the building. His eyes were a warm chestnut brown. They were nice to look at.

"Good morning, Freddie," I said with a smile.

He smiled back as he greeted me. "Hey, Conan."

He remembered my name!

"Sorry about last night. It's just that I've been dealing with Parker's shenanigans since we were kids."

"You don't need to apologize," I quickly said. "Thank you for asking Parker to be quieter."

"I told him to shut up, but I guess that's pretty much the same thing." He shrugged. "You're the new guy who moved in downstairs, right?"

I nodded.

"I may be a little late, but welcome to the building."

"Thank you."

Freddie glanced at my bag. "Are you heading to university?"

I nodded. "Bergson University."

When he smiled, his freckles danced on his face. "What a coincidence! I go there too. I'm heading there right now. Do you want to go together?"

I had a car, but I thought it would be nice to get to know Freddie, so I nodded. We got into his bright yellow buggy, and he drove down the road. Freddie told me more about himself. He was a year younger than me, just like Parker, and was born and raised in the Big City. He was a law student. When I told him that he must be very smart, his cheeks turned a beautiful shade of pink. Freddie said that he blushed easily and that it was a complex of his, but when I said that I thought it was a lovely complex, he blushed even more.

"Anyway, enough about me. Tell me about yourself," he said.

"My name is Conan."

Freddie laughed. "Something I don't know. What do you major in?"

"Philosophy."

"Hm, that's nice."

"Parker didn't seem to think the same."

Freddie rolled his eyes. "Parker is an idiot."

"I'm an idiot too," I said. Freddie scrunched his brows, so I added, "Parker told me so yesterday."

"Don't let him take advantage of your kindness. You have to show him that there are rules to follow and boundaries to respect. Anyway, are you new to the city?"

"Yes, I used to live in a small town that no one knows of."

"Why did you move away?"

"I wanted to leave my hometown."

"Too small for you?" he asked.

I shook my head. "Too big."

His eyes quirked up as he murmured, "I see… What did you do before coming here?"

"I took a year off to travel the world."

"Isn't the world a big place?" he asked with a smile.

"I think the world is too big for all of us."

Freddie laughed, although I didn't know why. "No wonder you major in philosophy. If you think the Big City is too big and need help finding your way around, you can knock at my door anytime."

"Does that mean we can be friends?" I asked hopefully. I think Freddie would have given me *The Look* if he wasn't looking straight ahead.

"Of course, we can be friends," he said softly.

Freddie was so nice. He handed me his phone and told me to type in my number. When he handed me the device, I made sure to be careful, so our fingers didn't touch. I didn't know much about law, and I didn't know what else to ask him, so I decided to ask him about Parker since we both knew him. Well, him more than me.

"How long have you been friends with Parker?" I asked.

He scoffed. "Friends? We're neighbors. But I've known him since elementary."

"Why does Parker drink and smoke?"

"It started when he was eighteen. He wasn't always that reckless before. He'd always been a flirt with a big ego, but the drinking, smoking, and reckless sex only started afterward."

"After what?" I asked curiously.

Freddie rubbed the back of his neck. "A tragic death."

I blinked in surprise but understood that Freddie didn't feel comfortable.

"Anyway, you might want to buy some earplugs. It won't be long before Parker starts getting noisy again. It'll only get worse now that college has started again."

"Why haven't you moved out?" I asked curiously.

He blinked, then scratched his chin with somewhat of a smile. "I ask myself that every day."

"I think you're a very nice person," I murmured.

"You do?"

"You look out for Parker."

Freddie ran his hand through his fluffy orange hair. "Someone has to look out for that shithead. Besides, I promised someone I would."

Freddie and I stopped talking about Parker. He told him more about himself, and I tried to do the same, but I thought listening to him was more interesting. Then we listened to the radio during the rest of the ride, and Freddie sang along to the music. He had such a pleasant singing voice.

"Seasons will change, and leaves will die,
but never you and I,

I won't let you go, not even in your tomb,
So, promise me you'll come back home."

Chapter 6: Universe-city

The university was big. Maybe that was why they called it "univers-ity." It felt like a small universe of its own, filled with its own population composed of students, professors, and adults. Foreigners were speaking all kinds of languages, and there were buildings for all sorts of subjects ranging from science to philosophy. This place was its own microcosm.

"You're a freshman, right?" Freddie asked, locking the car's doors.

"Yes."

Freddie looked around us before lowering his voice. "If anyone asks, tell them you're a senior. The students here like to pick on newcomers."

Freddie pursed his lips, looking at me from head to toe as if my small size worried him. "Be careful, okay? Hide if you have to."

"I'm good at hiding," I answered with a smile. I'd been hiding my entire life.

Freddie gave me *The Look*, but then smiled back. "Text me if anything happens. You have my number. I have to head to class now. I'll see you around."

I waved at him. "Goodbye, Freddie."

Freddie waved back before walking away. I saw him jog up to a group of students, most likely his friends, and the four walked towards a building while chatting and laughing.

I pulled out the school map I printed this morning. Despite having a map of the universe-city, I still got lost. I wasn't very good with directions. I went up to a few students who very kindly took the time to point out where the Philosophy building was, but I got lost again. I took a few seconds to stop and stare at the trees. Then, I noticed a group of students smoking near a trash can and went up to them.

"Hello, my name is Conan," I introduced myself with a wave. All three of them turned towards me. "Do you know where the Philosophy building is? I'm lost."

The blond boy pulled his cigarette away from his lips, which reminded me of Parker and how he smoked inside my apartment the first day I arrived. I'd been thinking about Parker a lot recently. How strange.

"Are you a first-year?" he asked, flicking the tip of his cigarette.

"Freddie said I have a master's degree," I told him.

The girl beside him snickered. "You're too young."

"Yes, I suppose," I murmured. Freddie didn't give me further indications, so I didn't know what else to say.

"How old are you?" one of them asked with bored eyes.

"Thank you for your help," I replied, which probably wasn't the right answer because they all simultaneously gave me *The Look*.

"Hey, wait," said the second boy when I turned to leave. "Why don't you stick around for a smoke?"

"No, thank you."

"Do you have any money?"

"I have a turkey sandwich."

The blond boy rolled his eyes and passed the cigarette to who I thought was his girlfriend until she started making out with the boy next to her. My stomach squirmed at the PDA, and I lowered my gaze.

"Lemme see your bag," he said.

"I can't," I told him. I had my journal inside, the one where I wrote everything I couldn't say aloud. I didn't want anyone to read it. Not even Dr. Philip George was allowed to see.

"So you *do* have money," he said, taking a step closer, which made me uncomfortable.

"I might have a penny," I murmured, feeling bad that I hadn't checked.

He took another step forward, and when I retreated, he seized my arm. I felt a jolt of electricity shoot up my limb, and my lungs tightened. My stomach curled, and I felt sick. Very sick. It felt like his skin was burning through the fabric of my sleeves. It hurt, but I tried to suppress the pain.

"Show me your bag," he ordered. I tried to say something, but I felt like my body was no longer connected to my mind, and all I could do was wait until he let go.

Just be patient, Conan. It'll be over soon. He can't hold you forever.

"What's wrong with him?" I heard the girl behind him snicker. "Maybe he doesn't speak English."

The tall boy laughed. "Do. You. Understand. Us?" he asked, making dramatic hand gestures that made his friends laugh harder. "Are. You. Stupid? Blink once for yes, blink twice for yes."

The three of them cracked up, bursting into mocking laughter.

"Hey, are you gonna open that bag for us or what?" The boy sneered, tightening his grip. I felt like the bones inside my flesh were going to snap, and my chest rose and fell unevenly.

"Seriously, what's wrong with him?" The girl scowled. "Ya think he's retarded?"

"Hey, dumbass, I said—"

"What's going on?" a husky voice demanded. Parker walked towards us; his motorcycle helmet tucked under his arm. His eyes narrowed at the hand gripping my arm before darting to the boy. An amused grin twisted on his beautiful face.

"I didn't know you were into dudes," he said mockingly. The boy's jaw tightened, and he immediately released my arm with a disgusted look.

"Fuck off," he sneered.

Parker took a step closer towards him, sizing him down with his intimidating height. "Listen carefully, shithead. If I ever catch you touching my boy again, I'll break every sturdy bone in your body. Understood?"

The boy clenched his fists but lowered his gaze, fear flashing in his eyes.

Parker reached out and took the pack of cigarettes from the boy's shirt pocket. "I'm confiscating this. Don't you know smoking is bad for you?" Parker said slyly, taking a cigarette out and placing it between his lips with a grin. He walked away, glancing over his shoulder and locking eyes with me, telling me to follow him. I quickly joined him and watched him light his cigarette.

"What were you thinking going up to them?" He sighed, and his dark eyes darted toward me. "Do you have a death wish or something?"

He looked at me with a hard expression and cold eyes, but he sounded worried.

"I was lost."

"And your plan was to go up to a bunch of delinquents?" he asked, sounding increasingly angry.

I stopped in my steps.

"What are you doing?" He backtracked and stopped in front of me, his eyebrows pulling together. "Why are you trembling?"

I lowered my head and stared at my feet, curling my fingers into fists. But I could still feel my body tremble. He reached out to touch me, but I whiffed my head, and he stopped. Parker understood that I didn't want to be touched and lowered his hand.

"I have problems," I croaked.

"Yeah, well, we all have fucking problems," he muttered, but his tone wasn't aggressive. "Shit, you're scaring me. Do you want some water?"

I shook my head. "I want to puke."

"You what?"

But I could already feel the three bites of toast and eggs travel up my throat, and before Parker had the chance to step away, I leaned forward and expelled my breakfast in front of me, meaning Parker's shoes. When I opened my eyes, there was brown mush on his shoes. It took me a few seconds to remember who and where I was. I looked up, and Parker had a scowl that looked like a scar.

"YOU'VE GOT TO BE KIDDING ME!"

Chapter 7: Physical Touch

I crouched in front of the boys' bathroom, quietly waiting for Parker to finish scrubbing his shoes in the sink. I could hear him mumbling angrily under his breath. I offered to help, but he strictly told me to stay away. He ordered me to leave, but I told him I wanted to stay by his side. He looked angry but told me to wait for him outside.

I didn't know what to do, so I texted my friend.

Me: Hello, Freddie. It's me, Conan. I hope you are doing well. I accidentally vomited on Parker's shoes. He is very upset. Do you think we can still be friends?

The sink stopped running, and a few seconds later, Parker came out of the bathroom in his socks. His sleeves were rolled up, revealing the veins traveling down his strong arms. He held his wet sneakers by their strings. He pretended like I wasn't there and marched away. I quietly followed him like a ghost.

"Go to class," I heard him say.

"Okay." I turned around to leave.

"Wait."

I stopped and glanced at him.

"Where are you going?" he asked.

"To class. You said—"

"I know what I said," he snapped. He let out a tired sigh, running a hand through his dark locks. "It doesn't mean I meant it."

I blinked. "Does that mean you want me to stay?"

"I'm *saying* that your professor won't let you in class, so you might as well stick with me."

That was Parker's way of asking me to stay.

"But keep a one-meter distance from me. I don't want you to puke on my socks," he warned me.

"Okay."

We continued to walk in silence, but a student rushed past us. I didn't want to break the one-meter rule, so I didn't step aside, and our shoulders collided. I lost my balance, falling on my bum.

"Hey, watch it!" the student snapped at me.

"I'm sorry," I replied. The student was about to leave, but Parker grabbed his arm. The student blinked in surprise, his expression turning from annoyance to fear when his gaze met Parker's.

"Apologize to Dandelion," Parker ordered.

"Who?"

"Him. The idiot who fell on the floor," Parker said, nodding towards me.

The student looked at me and then at Parker, who was two heads taller. The student then turned towards me and mumbled, "Sorry, Dandelion."

I smiled. "My name is Conan. It's nice to meet you."

Parker rolled his eyes and released the student who scurried away.

"What are you doing?" Parker demanded.

"Breathing."

He looked at me in despair.

"No, I mean why did you apologize when it wasn't your fault?" Parker asked, trying not to sound upset. When I didn't answer, Parker crouched down in front of me and leaned forward. He broke the one-meter rule, and his nose was inches away from mine. He looked at me, his black eyes drilling into my gaze. I couldn't help but think: what beautiful stones of onyx he has. He was probably thinking, *what an idiot.*

He sighed. "Do you always let people push you around?"

"I don't think the boy did it on purpose. When people are upset, I tell myself they must be having a bad day. I don't think humans are bad by nature."

Parker's head fell forward, and he exhaled loudly. His dark hair fell over his forehead, and I couldn't see the expression on his face.

"Idiot," he mumbled softly under his breath.

He stood up and walked away. I scrambled onto my feet and followed him, but he slowed his pace, and I was no longer behind Parker, but beside him.

We continued down the hall in silence. A group of students walked towards us, and as they got closer, Parker grabbed my sleeve and pulled me towards him. He kept me on his right side, between him and the wall, so no one would bump into me. People made way for Parker, gluing their backs to the other side of the wall. The guys seemed intimidated by his presence while the girls cast him flirty looks and smiles, but Parker remained indifferent.

"Thank you," I said. I knew he had heard me, but he didn't reply. Maybe he was still upset about his shoes.

We stopped in an empty hallway that had open windows. Parker put his shoes on the ledge to let them dry under the sun. There was something eye-catching about the way the sun hit his features.

"You're very handsome," I told him.

He scowled. "Don't be a creep."

"Oh, I'm sorry."

Parker stared at me, opened his mouth, then closed it. Instead of calling me an idiot, he let out a small sigh. I didn't know if he was angry at me. Maybe Parker had problems communicating, like I did.

"I don't always mean what I say, so don't take everything to heart. My temper sometimes gets the better of me," he said, which seemed to be Parker's way of apologizing. I had a hard time understanding people, but strangely, Parker was easy to understand.

"Okay."

Parker nodded once and lit a cigarette. He handed it to me, but I shook my head. He shrugged, bringing it to his lips and taking a drag. I admired his sharp jaw and cheekbones.

People who killed themselves publicly fascinated me. If you thought about it, smoking was a socially accepted way to slowly kill yourself.

I thought it was interesting how smoking was romanticized. Unconsciously, or perhaps consciously, we romanticized death. We thought about it constantly. We were obsessed with it, were surrounded by it, one way or another, death was omnipresent in our lives, yet we rarely ever spoke about it. Humans were a paradox.

"Tell me something about yourself," Parker said, his cigarette still dangling between his lips.

"What would you like to know?" It was one of the rare but precious moments someone took an interest in my existence.

"You said you had problems earlier. What kind of problems do you have?"

I squeezed my hands together. "I can't tell you. My therapist said I shouldn't tell anyone unless I'm ready."

"You have a therapist?" he asked, but he didn't seem surprised.

"Yes."

"Wow, you must be fucked up in the head." He laughed grimly. But again, it didn't sound like an insult, but as if he was stating a fact. "It's fine, you don't have to tell me. I was only tryna make small talk, anyway."

"Can I ask you a question?"

"Shoot."

"Was the girl you were with last night your lover?"

My question made Parker laugh. He flicked the tip of his cigarette, and the flakes of ash fell on the window ledge. I gently brushed them away.

"She was a one-night stand," he said flatly.

"You're not in love with her?"

"God, no. I make love to her. That's it."

"What do you like about making love to someone?" I asked, genuinely curious. I hoped that Parker, who seemed experienced in that field, could enlighten me and explain the perks of sexual pleasure. My mind could never comprehend it. Like the rest of the world, it was an enigma.

"People are vulnerable during sex," he finally said, and he didn't add anything else.

"Do you have someone you love?" I asked.

The expression on Parker's face darkened. "Yeah, I did."

Did.

"What about you?" he asked.

"I don't think I'm capable of love."

"Why not? Did you get your heart broken?" He smirked.

"Oh no, a lot of things are broken, but strangely not my heart. I have quite a healthy heart actually. It beats between 60 and 100bpm." I paused. "Except for when I run."

Parker stared at me. I must have said something strange again.

"I just can't love," I concluded. "And even if it was possible, I'm leaving in a year."

Parker rested his elbow against the window frame, leaning his chin on his palm while the cigarette burned between his fingers. His piercing gaze softened slightly, but even under the light, his eyes were black.

"Where are you heading?"

"I don't know."

"Sounds like a nice place."

I nodded in agreement.

"But if I was normal, and could develop normal feelings, and lived a normal life, I think I'd fall for someone like you."

I must have said something that creeped him out again. His eyes widened, and an expression I couldn't read crossed his face. He turned his head the other way, and I could no longer see his face. I frowned, feeling wistful. I didn't want our conversation to end.

"You don't like it when people touch you, right?" he asked, clearing his voice.

"No, I get sick."

"Then there's no chance that you and I will ever get together," he said firmly, his gaze finally meeting mine. "I don't date people I can't fuck."

"Can we still be friends?" I asked, my voice full of hope.

He shrugged lazily. "Doesn't matter to me."

I think that was Parker's way of saying yes, so I smiled. His eyes were a beautiful shade of liquid black. Even if it was only the second time we'd talked, I felt like I slowly starting to understand him. After all, he and I weren't so different.

"Would it kill you if I touched you?" he suddenly asked.

My smile faded, and my heart ached, and suddenly, the lack of distance between us made me self-conscious and uncomfortable. I didn't realize how close we were standing until now, with less than a meter between us.

"It would," I answered, in spite of myself.

Parker nodded. "Shame." And he continued to smoke the rest of his cigarette in silence.

Chapter 8: By Chance

Freddie bent forward, clutching his stomach as he burst into laughter. He joined us after his class ended, and I had just finished telling him what had happened. His eyes shifted to Parker and he chuckled, wiping away his tears. "Serves you right for always being a jerk."

"I didn't mean to dirty his shoes," I murmured.

"It doesn't matter. My shoes are still dirty," Parker snapped.

"I'm—"

He shot me a glare. "Don't you dare apologize again."

"Okay."

"Parker, can't you be nicer?" Freddie sighed.

"Oh, you mean to the guy who ruined my favorite pair of shoes?" Parker said.

I felt guilty and was about to apologize, but I remembered that Parker didn't like it when I did, so I remained silent. Freddie lectured Parker for letting his temper get the better of him, but Parker quickly lost interest, his eyes lingering on a group of girls that walked past us. His dark eyes rested on their swaying hips.

"Are you even listening?" Freddie snapped.

"Absolutely," Parker replied.

I turned towards the window, blinking in surprise when one of Parker's shoes was missing.

"Parker, a bird stole your shoe," I murmured.

"Is that some kind of philosophical metaphor?"

I shook my head and pointed out the window at the large bird that swooped down and stole one of his sneakers.

"Look. A bird is flying away with your shoe," I said.

Parker followed the direction of my finger, his eyes widening when he saw that his shoe was dangling in mid-air, hanging from the talons of what looked like an eagle.

"Do you know how expensive those shoes are?!" he cried, outraged. He stuck his head out the window and started yelling, "Hey, dumb fucker! Fly back here with my shoe!"

The bird pooped, and Freddy couldn't control his laughter.

"I don't think it speaks English," I told him.

"That shithead," Parker sneered. He turned towards me. "Conan, hand me a notebook so I can throw it at the bird."

"Okay." I opened my bag and handed him my brand-new notebook.

Before Parker could throw it, Freddie snatched it out of his hand. "You are not throwing Conan's notebook out the window!" Freddie hissed, putting it back into my bag and zipping it shut.

"Dandelion, hand me the notebook," Parker ordered, giving out his hand. I was about to open my bag, but Freddie stopped me.

"No, don't give it to him."

"Conan doesn't mind!" Parker growled.

"Because he's too nice to say no!"

"Conan, if you're my friend, you'll give me the notebook."

"Conan, if you're *my* friend, you won't give him your notebook."

"You're not his friend," Parker snapped.

"I am. He said so himself when we drove here."

"Yeah, well, if Dandelion wasn't a weirdo, he said he'd date me," Parker huffed proudly.

"How is that even relevant?"

The bird let go of the laces, and I watched the shoe fall from the sky. It looked like a mini comet.

"The bird dropped your shoe," I said.

"We don't need any more philosophical metaphors," Parker groaned.

Freddy snorted. "It's not a metaphor. The bird really dropped your shoe."

"Where did it land?"

"That building over there," I told him, pointing at it.

"That son of a..." Parker continued to mutter under his breath. He ran down the hall in his socks but stopped, glancing over his shoulder. "Well? Are you two coming or not?"

"Yeah, yeah, I'm coming," Freddie said.

I smiled. "Me too!" I took off my shoes and ran after them in my socks. I'd always wanted to run outside without my shoes.

We ran across campus and made it to the Science building. We climbed the stairs, but I was out of breath when we reached the second floor. I was never very athletic, and since my body was weaker than most, I'd always sit out during gym class for medical reasons. I'd spend the hour with my female classmates who, for some reason, rarely participated in gym class.

Tired, I crouched down.

"What are you doing?" Parker asked when he saw that I had stopped. Before I could answer, he said, "Besides breathing."

"Resting."

"This isn't the time to be resting!"

"But my legs hurt."

Parker threw his hands in the air in despair and turned towards Freddie. Freddie asked if I needed help getting up, but I shook my head.

"I'll help you up," Freddy insisted gently, extending his hand. My chest tightened when he stood so close, but Parker pushed his hand away.

"He doesn't like touching people," he said firmly, protectively standing between us.

Freddie frowned. "Okay, we'll wait. Take your time," he said in a calm and understanding voice.

Freddie was so nice, I wanted to cry. But that would be weird, so I didn't.

"Thank you."

When the dizziness went away, we continued our journey up the flight of stairs. The door to the rooftop was locked, but Parker picked at it with a bobby pin he kept in his pocket. Freddy rolled his eyes when the latch clicked, but I stared at Parker with wide eyes.

"Why are you looking at me like that?" he demanded.

"You're amazing," I told him.

He blinked in surprise and quickly looked the other way. "So fucking weird," I heard him mutter under his breath. He spoke in a harsh tone, but I think he was blushing.

Parker pushed open the door, and a gentle gust of wind greeted us when we walked onto the roof. We leaned over the metal rail that protected the extremities. Parker's shoe was on the ledge below us. It was out of arm's reach.

"How about I grab one of you by the ankle?" Parker suggested.

"You are not dangling one of us over the roof ledge," Freddie said sternly.

Parker ignored him and turned towards me. "Come on, dandelion, I'll dangle you over the ledge."

"Parker!" Freddy cried in a mother's voice whenever a child said something absurd.

"What? I need my shoe!"

"And Conan needs to live!"

Not really. But I kept the thought to myself.

"I'm sorry, Parker, I can't do it," I said.

Parker looked at me and must have remembered that I had problems. I wouldn't be able to handle the physical contact if he touched my ankles. Parker didn't insist and ran a frustrated hair through his hair.

"Redhead, you're my last hope."

"I am not risking my life for your smelly shoe."

"The shoe has sentimental value," Parker glowered.

Freddie snorted. "Sentimental value?"

"Not the shoe, the shoelace."

Freddy cocked a brow, and his voice took a mocking tone. "Did one of your one-night stands give it to you?"

"No, my dead boyfriend did."

Parker's tone was flat, but he did it to mask the pain his eyes failed to hide. He took a deep breath, and I could tell he was distressed and truly upset about his shoe. Or rather, his shoelace. He ran another hand through his hair before letting it fall to his side.

"I'll give up sex for a week," Parker finally said.

Freddie crossed his arms over his chest. "A month."

"Two weeks. And that is already asking for a lot."

"Deal," Freddie replied.

"Dandelion, hold this for me," Parker said, shoving his jacket against my chest. His jacket was heavy and smelled strongly of cigarettes and men's cologne, but his body's warmth lingered on the fabric, and I wanted to wrap it around myself like a blanket.

"Be careful, and don't drop Freddie. He might crack his skull on the concrete and die," I said.

They simultaneously turned towards me and gave me *The Look.*

Freddy climbed over the ledge, and Parker grabbed his ankles. I wondered if this was what other adults did during their free time. Freddie crawled over the ledge and pressed the palm of his hands against the building wall while Parker carefully lowered him. You could see the veins in Parker's biceps when his muscles contracted, and the muscles near his chest became more prominent.

"Can you reach it?" Parker winced; his jaw tight.

"Not yet. Lower me more, will you?" we heard Freddie say from below. Parker tried to lower him, but he leaned forward too much and lost his balance. I quickly wrapped my arms around his waist so he wouldn't fall. My chest pressed against his broad back, and I could feel his tense muscles. The pang of nausea made my stomach curl, and my fingers dug into his clothes. I didn't want my friends to die.

"I think I'm going to puke," I announced weakly, squeezing my eyes shut.

"Hold it in, dandelion," Parker warned me. "Don't let me go."

Parker was asking me for two arduous tasks. I clutched onto his shirt nonetheless, trying to suppress the pain. I wanted to let Parker go so badly, but I held onto him.

"I got it!" we heard Freddie exclaim.

"What are you boys doing?!" shouted someone from below. A large group of people, mostly students, were filming us from below, gasping and murmuring in shock. Two students dangling someone over the roof must look sketchy without context. A scary-looking man rushed into the science building.

"Reel me back before the supervisor gets here," Freddie ordered. Parker and I, but mostly Parker, pulled him back onto the roof. Freddie's face was as bright as a tomato, and he hugged the ground with Parker's shoe in his hand. My body was shaking, and the pain in my chest was unbearable. I wanted to laugh and cry.

The door flung open, and the supervisor stormed towards us. "What in the name of tartar sauce are your boys doing?! If this is some kind of sick college prank, I swear..."

But the three of us were too busy laughing ourselves silly. My body erupted with relief and fear. It was the first time I felt even a fraction of happiness while suffering. Their laughter collided with mine, and together we created a beautiful symphony filled with joy, youth, and relief. Wasn't it beautiful? In a life that held a billion possibilities, the Universe had aligned my fate with two people who made the world a little less lonely and much more wonderful.

Chapter 9: Zev the Candy Man

Dear,

This is the first time I'm writing in my journal since arriving in the Big City. It's been a little over a week since university started. So far, my first few classes have been great. The philosophy professor is an old, strict man, but he's very wise. He's so wise that we sometimes can't understand him. I don't think anyone in this lifetime can.

It's lunchtime now, and I'm writing in my journal, so I don't have to eat. Everything has been going well, but my stomach still isn't cooperating. But I'm trying. I really am.

Parker has kept his promise. It's been a week since he's stopped making love. I know this because I haven't heard any banging or moaning from above. Freddie told me Parker had commitment issues ever since his ex-boyfriend passed away, so I wasn't sure if Parker would keep his promise. But he did, and I felt guilty for doubting him. I apologized to him when I saw him in the parking lot. He scowled, saying it was "too early for this sh*t," and walked away. He's been more agitated and aggressive since he's stopped making love, which seemed to be his coping mechanism, but

Freddie told me not to worry. Freddie seemed more worried about me.

There is something sad about Parker. He carries grief in his eyes and exhaustion beneath them. Freddie said Parker has never been the same after his ex-boyfriend's death, and said he turned to drinking, smoking, and empty sex to help him forget. When I asked how he had died, Freddie didn't answer, but I could tell that whatever the reason was, it saddened him deeply.

Freddie and I often go home together, which gives us lots of time to talk. I'm happy that I can use the word "home." Even though it's only a temporary place to live, there's something heartwarming about a place you can call yours. The Dark Thoughts haven't been bothering me for now. Though, I still feel lonely. It's strange. There are over seven billion people on Earth, yet we feel lonely. Or maybe it's just me. Anyway, I'm going to try to finish my sandwich. I'll write again soon.

Yours truly

I closed my journal and carefully put it inside my bag. I couldn't finish my sandwich, so I put it in a plastic Ziplock before heading to class. As I walked down the hall, I saw Parker flirting with a brown-haired girl, one that I'd never seen him with before. I wanted to wave at him, but I stopped in my steps when he leaned forward to kiss the girl. It wasn't a peck on the lips but an adult kiss, and when I saw the pink color of Parker's tongue enter her mouth while his hand scaled down her back, I immediately felt sick. Parker's eyes then met mine, and I felt an electric shock shoot down my spine from the intensity of his gaze. His eyebrows furrowed, and I began to panic. I turned on my heel and ran away.

I went into the nearest bathroom. My stomach burned, and my throat ached, and I ended up hurling what little food I had eaten. I rinsed my mouth and washed my face. I wobbled out of the bathroom and stopped beside the entrance, staring at the floor. If I passed out now, I'd wake up in a hospital, and then Dr. Philip George would send me away.

"Are you okay?" asked a voice. I wondered if it was God. I raised my head, and a tall boy with milk chocolate skin stood in front of me. His thick but groomed eyebrows pulled together in worry. He looked perplexed but so very handsome.

"Hello. Sorry. My name is Conan." The words came out all jumbled, and I felt like the hours I spent practicing in front of the mirror had gone to waste. The boy laughed, and I gaped at his pearly white teeth.

"Hey. It's okay. I'm Zev." He smiled coolly. "You look kind of pale."

"I feel sick."

"Do you want to sit down?" he asked, looking around to see if there were any chairs. My legs felt like noodles, so I sat on the floor.

He chuckled, sitting beside me. "Or we can do that."

He was too close, so I scooted away from him. He noticed but didn't ask or come any closer. I felt grateful.

"Here," Zev said, taking something out from his pocket. It was a lollipop.

"No, thank you," I politely declined.

"Not a fan of lollipops? I have some toffee if you want."

He took out a handful of candy and opened his palm, letting me choose. I chose the coffee-flavored toffee, which he said was his favorite. The sugar chased away the dizziness, and I felt a little better.

"I have a sweet tooth," Zev explained, popping candy into his mouth. "What about you? What do you like?"

"I like philosophy," I told him.

"Are you a philosophy major?"

I nodded. The smile on his face widened, and the corner of his eyes wrinkled.

"Then we must have a couple of classes together. I have a double major in law and philosophy. Do you have classes with Mr. Flent?"

"The wise man no one can understand?"

Zev laughed. His husky voice sounded like music.

"Yes, that's the one."

"Oh, then yes! Do you know Freddie? He studies law," I told him.

His lips puckered sideways, and he seemed to be deep in thought.

"Freddie," he hummed. "Do you have his last name?"

"No, but I have his phone number."

Zev laughed. His laugh was different from Freddie's. It was louder and bouncier, the contagious type that made you want to laugh along with him.

"What's he like?" he asked.

"He has brown eyes, freckles, and bright orange hair. Parker sometimes calls him Chucky."

"Oh, you mean the cute boy with freckles?" Zev asked. "Yeah, I know him. Well, I know *of* him. We have a couple of classes together, but I've never had the chance to talk to him. He seems nice. Smart too."

I smiled. "He's my friend."

He chuckled softly. "I'm glad he is."

"Would you like to be his friend too?"

"I'd love to."

Zev asked if he and I could exchange numbers, so we did. He asked me if I had any social media, but I said I didn't. He shrugged, telling me I didn't look like the type to have one. I didn't know what he meant by that, so I thanked him, and then he laughed, and so did I, and it was all very nice.

"Do you feel better?" he asked.

"Yes, thank you."

"Distracting feelings with thoughts always helps," he said, which was when I realized that he had been asking me plenty of questions to distract me from nausea.

"Thank you, Zev. I'd shake your hand if I could."

"You can't?"

"I get sick when I touch people."

"We can still shake hands."

I didn't understand what he meant until he told me to extend my hand. When I did, so did he. Our hands didn't touch, but we shook the air as if we were really shaking our hands. We both looked at each other and laughed. I wished I had met Zev earlier in my life.

"So, did you eat something bad for lunch or...?"

"Oh no, I saw Parker kiss someone," I replied simply.

Zev blinked in surprise. "Parker?"

"Do you know him?"

"He's quite popular here. Do you like him?" Zev asked.

"Yes, of course."

"Do you think he's handsome?"

I nodded. "Very."

"Have you ever thought about sleeping with him?"

"No, never," I blurted in horror. The thought of lying naked in bed with his dangerous body disgusted and excited me. I wrapped my arms around my uneasy stomach. Zev saw the pain in my face and frowned.

"Sorry, I must have asked something too personal. It's just when people talk about him, it's mostly about... You know."

"Making love?"

"Yes, making love," he murmured.

"Parker and I are friends. I told him I couldn't love, and he told me he wouldn't date someone he can't sleep with," I explained.

Zev nodded. "Well, that's good. You'd probably get hurt if you fell for him. All the girls here do. They think they're the one for him, that they're different, and that they can change his bad manners and self-destructive behavior. I don't understand why they romanticize his toxic behavior. They throw themselves at his feet and try to fix him."

"Parker isn't a bad person," I murmured.

"No, but he's not the first person you'd go to for a healthy and sustainable relationship."

"He's not a bad person," I repeated. "I don't believe people are bad by nature. I think Parker is hurt. He's hurt so much that he can't do good, and that just proves how much he suffers. Being bad isn't a principle—it's a consequence. Maybe the girls failed to fix him because nothing about him needs fixing. You can't fix the essence of existence—that would contradict the laws of nature. Parker simply needs to find who he once was. The good Parker. The happy one."

Zev looked at me, his lips slightly parted. "A real philosopher. You're going to write amazing essays one day, Conan."

"I don't think I will."

"Why not?"

"I can't write if—"

Zev's phone began to ring.

"Shoot, I have to get this. Girlfriend alert." He gave me a quick smile. "You don't mind?"

"No, of course not. Your girlfriend is more important. Please say hi to her for me. My name is Conan."

He laughed. "I will."

I waved at him, and he handed me a handful of candy.

"Don't tell your dentist," he whispered, as if it was a secret only between him and me. I looked down at the candy and smiled.

Three friends, can you believe that?

Chapter 10: Drunk on Life

I heard a door slam shut, and my eyes flung open. Heavy footsteps followed the noise like an elephant trudging above my ceiling. I thought I'd imagined it at first, that I was tired, but then I heard glass breaking and knew I wasn't dreaming. I climbed out of bed and left the comfort of my bed, heading upstairs. I knocked on Parker's door and called his name.

"Parker?"

No answer. I pressed my ear against the flat surface and could hear someone puking, which I guess was some form of an answer.

I twisted the doorknob and said, "I'm coming in," even though he probably couldn't hear me. My nose wrinkled as soon as I walked in. The stench of cigarettes and alcohol invaded my nostrils. His house was dark, but I could see empty bottles aligned against the wall. Some were empty, but none of them were full. It looked like a tornado came in and destroyed everything. The furniture was flipped over, books were scattered across the floor, and shattered glass glistened under the dim light. I followed the noise of vomiting, which led me to the bathroom. Parker was crouched in front of the toilet, expelling the content inside his stomach.

"Good evening, Parker."

He looked up, breathing heavily. His complexion had gone ghostly pale. I looked into his eyes, and it was like staring into an endless depth of ink, sorrow, and pain.

He groaned miserably, leaning his back against the tub and sliding onto the floor. "Get out," he hissed, his voice scratchy and ragged.

"Parker, you can't sleep here," I said, but he wouldn't open his eyes. I picked up a toothbrush and poked his hollow cheek. "Parker, wake up. You'll catch a cold."

His eyes flung open with anger. "Parker this, Parker that—stop telling me what to do!" he barked, pushing me away. I stumbled back and fell on my bum. His eyebrows furrowed in worry, and he was about to reach out to help me, but he stopped himself. "So fucking weak," he muttered, wiping his lips with the back of his hand.

"I'm sorry."

"Stop apologizing! It's not your goddamn fault!"

"But you're upset."

"What does that matter to you?!" he shouted. His face went from ghostly pale to Freddie red.

"You're my friend. Of course, you matter."

Parker dragged his hand miserably down his face and spat, "Get out."

"I don't want you to die."

His voice rose. "We're all fucking dying!"

"I know."

Freddie told me that Parker could get violent on his worst nights.

"Just go. I don't want you to see me like this."

"Everything is more beautiful because we are doomed. You will never be lovelier than you are now. We will never be here again."

Parker narrowed his eyes. "What?"

"It's a quote by Homer from *The Iliad*," I explained.

"I'm too drunk for your philosophical shit. Just go," he growled.

I stood up, but Parker quickly caught my hand when I did. My body stiffened at his touch, and I tried to pull away, but he wouldn't let me go. The Parker in front of me wasn't the Parker I knew. The normal Parker would have released me. He was a different Parker. The drunk and angry Parker. The one who wouldn't let me go.

"Wait," he whispered. His warm hands felt like magma, and I wanted so badly to pull away. My lungs felt clogged, and I felt like I couldn't breathe.

"Parker—"

His dark eyes drilled into my gaze, bleeding with pain. "Would you hate me if I held you?" he asked, sounding almost desperate. His husky voice and intense gaze aroused me. Excitement and pain coursed through me. I felt increasingly sick and aroused, and the two clashing emotions felt overwhelming. I shook my head silently, trying to remain calm.

Stay still and wait until it's over. It'll end eventually, Conan. It always does.

"No, I could never hate you, but I would never forgive you," I murmured, staring at his hand still wrapped around my thin wrist.

When my gaze met his eyes, he let me go. He looked at me, noticing how badly I was shaking, and swore under his breath. His face fell into his hands, and his jaw tightened.

"I didn't mean to hurt you, dandelion." His voice broke with regret. "Fuck, I can't think properly. I'm too drunk."

He peered at me, guilt swimming in his dark eyes. He tried to compose himself before speaking again. "Go home before I do something stupid again," he murmured.

"Okay, but you should go to bed first. It's cold here."

"It's always cold."

His voice was empty, and his eyes were unfocused. He clutched onto the tub to help himself up. The movement made the muscles in his arms more prominent, which reminded me how much stronger Parker was. He could have hurt me if he wanted to. Parker wobbled to his room, and I followed his staggering steps. His room was the only place that didn't smell of alcohol and cigarettes. Parker collapsed onto the bed, and I stood at the doorframe.

"Did you come back from a party?" I asked.

He was quiet for a second, and I thought he had fallen asleep.

"Yes."

"Did you drive your motorcycle?"

"Yes, mother, I drove my motorcycle."

I frowned. "I'm not your mother."

"It was a joke, dandelion."

"My name is Conan."

I expected him to scowl and call me an idiot, but instead, his eyes softened, and the tiniest smile turned upon his lips.

"I like calling you dandelion, that's all."

"Why?"

He didn't answer. I read in a book that close friends gave each other nicknames. Parker sometimes called Freddie "Chucky," and Freddie sometimes called Parker an addict. I tried to think of a nickname for Parker.

"Can I call you Park?" I asked.

He deadpanned. "If you do, we're no longer friends."

"Oh, okay." I guess Parker didn't like nicknames. That was fine. I liked his name anyway.

"Did you drive drunk?" I asked. The number of questions that popped into my mind surprised me. I normally had to search for questions to keep a conversation going, but with Parker, they came naturally. I wondered what was so different about him.

There was a long pause.

"Yeah," he admitted. I felt a knife twist into my chest.

"Don't do it again, okay? Don't drive when you're drunk."

He sighed heavily. "Why do you care?" And when I didn't answer, he said, "If you don't know, then stop."

"I can't."

"Of course, you can."

But I shook my head. "I can't. I can't because you're my friend. You're already here and here," I said, pointing to my heart. "Freddie, too. He's here and here."

I shifted my finger an inch away from Parker's spot. Parker turned his back towards me.

"So fucking stupid," but his voice was soft. Parker swore when he was flustered.

"Why did you drive drunk?" I asked. It was the first time I had so many questions that weren't written in books on how to socialize.

There was a long pause, and then he finally spoke.

"Swallowing vodka is easier than remembering."

His voice was raw and full of pain, but he tried to keep it as light as possible.

"I'd rather burn my throat and blackout with a hangover than spend hours thinking about someone who's gone. The worst part is that I drink and smoke until four a.m. loving him, and I wake up with a headache still in love with him. He's gone, but I'm stuck here, and the feelings are the same."

Beneath his leather jacket and condescending smirks, Parker was heartbroken. I didn't know what to say to comfort him. Perhaps there was nothing I could say that would make him feel better.

"I drove drunk because I wanted to see him again."

The room fell silent. Parker fell asleep, and I was alone. His house was a mess, and I did something terrible. I went to my apartment room and grabbed a garbage bag. I returned to Parker's house and threw away every substance that could kill him. No, that was killing him. The alcohol, the cigarettes, the crushed powder, and the pills, everything that made me want to cry. I heaved the garbage bag outside, recycled the plastic and threw away the bottles in the green trash. It wasn't until I returned to bed that I started crying. I shouldn't have touched Parker's stuff without his permission. He was going to hate me for wasting his money, for doing something without his permission, but I was so upset, I couldn't stop myself.

I cried because I was upset. I cried because I was crying. I cried because Parker was sad. I cried because he could have died in so many ways, knowing that if he was still here, asleep and not dead, it was only because fate had mercy and spared him one more day. And then I stopped crying because I was tired. I remembered how he held my hand in the bathroom, and despite the nauseous feeling, I wanted to hold his hand a little longer. That had never happened before. I curled into a ball and hugged my knees against my chest, putting a hand against my racing heart where Parker and Freddie were, and I fell asleep dreaming of dandelions.

Chapter 11: Three Merry Friends

I woke up early in the morning and got ready for class. I picked up my bag and headed upstairs to Freddie's house. We went to school together. I knocked on his door and smiled when he stepped out. "Good morning, Freddie. How are you?"

"I'm okay," he replied, rubbing his eyes.

"You don't look okay. You look tired."

He blinked, then let out a sheepish laugh. "You're right. I'm doing terrible. I spent the entire night working on an essay due in two weeks. It counts for 60% of my grade, and it's stressing me out." He sighed. "But thank you for asking how I'm doing."

"Everyone asks how the other is doing," I said, having read it in multiple books.

Freddie shook his head with a small smile. "Not the way you do."

As we were about to leave, Parker's door opened. He wore sunglasses that hid half his face, and only his strong jaw and chin were visible. He ran a quick hand through his bedroom hair. The dark tints of his glasses matched his leather jacket and his natural sex appeal, but it wasn't sunny outside. It was rather gray today. Despite the dark tints that hid his eyes,

I could feel him staring at me intently. I was worried that he'd get mad at me. He must have noticed by now that many of his belongings were gone and that the culprit was me.

Instead, he said, "I was hoping to catch you two." His voice was huskier than usual.

"Why?" Freddie asked, raising a brow.

"Aren't you two heading to uni?"

"Yeah," Freddie replied.

"Great, then the three of us can go together like the merry friends we are," Parker said.

"What about your motorcycle?"

"The alcohol from last night is still running through my system. To be honest, I'm seeing three of you," Parker answered casually. "Besides, I promised Dandelion I wouldn't kill myself on the road. Now let's go. I have a biology test to ace."

Before Freddie could say anything, Parker headed downstairs, whistling a cheerful tune.

Freddie made a funny noise with his nose. "The audacity."

We followed Parker downstairs and went to Freddie's car. I usually sat in the front, but I thought it was normal to let Parker sit there since he was taller. The front seat had more space for his long legs. I sat in the back, but when I did, so did he.

"Don't you want to sit beside Freddie?" I asked.

He scowled at me. "What kind of stupid question is that?"

"I'm this close to kicking you out of my car," Freddie warned him.

"Love you too, babe."

Parker took off his jacket, revealing his starch white shirt and sturdy chest. He pulled up his sleeves that showed the muscles and veins in his arms. I looked away, feeling fuzzy.

The drive to school was quiet. I told them that I had made a new friend named Zev, and Parker remained silent while Freddie seemed happy for me. I told Freddie that Zev had called him "the cute boy with freckles," and he immediately flushed red. We almost crashed into the car in front of us. And then we arrived at our university.

"I have to get going. I have to print the rest of my papers before class starts. I'll see you guys!" Freddie said, giving us a quick wave before running off. Without Freddie, the atmosphere shifted. I guess this is what people called an awkward silence.

"What class do you have?" Parker asked, breaking the silence.

"Philosophy," I answered.

"Building C, right?"

"I wouldn't know."

Parker ran a hand through his dark hair, looking both amused and annoyed, and sighed. "Of course."

Parker looked around, and his eyes stopped on two girls. He stopped them in their tracks and began talking with them. The girls suddenly started touching their hair and giggling. They seemed to know who Parker was, but it didn't go the other way around. Despite not knowing them, Parker seemed at ease. While the girls struggled to keep eye contact,

Parker stood there, confident and unwavering. He was aware of his appeal and was indifferent to the compliments.

"Do you girls have a cigarette?" Parker asked.

"Oh, yes, I think I do." Both girls began rummaging through their bags as if racing to see who could get Parker a cigarette first. The brunette won, and she quickly handed Parker a cigarette. He set it between his lips and leaned forward, letting her light the tip. He asked for directions, and they told him.

"Thanks for the info and the cigarette."

"Don't you want to stay a little longer? Class doesn't start until another thirty minutes," the blond girl said. Her eyes kept darting toward Parker's brawny arms.

"Someone's waiting for me."

"Your girlfriend?" asked the brunette with a frown, disappointment flashing through her eyes.

Parker took a drag from his cigarette, then turned towards me. The girls followed his gaze, and they seemed confused, relieved, and annoyed when they saw me. I smiled and waved at them.

"No, a friend," Parker said solemnly.

The girls tried to convince Parker to stay, but he seemed distracted, focusing on me as he finished his cigarette. They finally gave up, but they gave Parker their numbers in case he changed his mind. Parker came back to me, tossing his cigarette bud aside.

"The girls over there said that philosophy majors have class in building C. Let's go."

"Just a second, please."

I crouched down and picked up his cigarette bud. I pressed the burning ashes against the concrete to make sure the fire was completely out and waited a few seconds just to be completely sure before throwing it in a cigarette receptacle.

"Okay, I'm ready," I announced with a smile.

Parker stood there, staring at me in silence. It was hard to tell what he was thinking.

"Is something wrong?" I asked.

"I was just thinking," he replied, his voice distant.

"About what?"

"About how you're too good for this world."

He walked away, and I scurried after him, doubling my pace just to match his.

"You're good at making friends," I told him.

"You mean the two girls at the parking lot? They're not my friends."

"They aren't?"

He shrugged, slowing his pace when he noticed my struggle. "No, they're two people who just so happen to know where the philosophy building is. And perhaps girls I'll eventually sleep with, but definitely not friends. I keep my friend circle small."

He smiled at me, which sharpened his features. "Surprised that a jackass like me values friends?"

"No, not a bit."

Parker's smile slowly vanished, and he looked straight ahead, shoving his hands into his jacket pockets. "Then you're the first."

We walked in silence afterward. I had the feeling that Parker wanted to tell me something, that he had a lot on his mind but couldn't find the words to express his thoughts. That often happened to me too, so I decided not to say anything and let him think. I enjoyed walking in silence anyway. His presence was enough.

He walked me to class, and we stopped at the door.

"Hey, dandelion?"

I looked at him. I'd never seen Parker nervous. Well, not until now anyway. He ran his hand through his hair and let it fall to the nape of his neck.

"I'm sorry about last night," he finally said.

"It's fine."

"No, it's not. I said and did a lot of stupid things, and worst of all, I hurt you," he mumbled.

"I don't think your sadness is stupid."

Parker's jaw tightened, looking away for an instant before turning back towards me.

"Can we forget what happened last night? I don't remember everything that happened, but I wouldn't be surprised if I talked about..." His voice drifted away, and he dismissed the unfinished sentence with an "anyway." A pause. "You'll forget about it, right?"

"I don't know if I can forget what happened."

He flinched.

"I wish I could, but I don't think my brain would cooperate," I explained. "But I can avoid bringing it up if you'd like."

Parker gave me a small smile. "Yeah, that works too."

"I'm sorry for throwing away your alcohol and cigarettes. I was upset."

"It's fine. I would have done the same."

"Thank you for forgiving me. I'm glad we're friends. I have to go now. Goodbye, Parker." I waved and was about to leave. He reached out to stop me but quickly curled his fingers and retrieved his hand.

"Dandelion?" he called instead. I stopped in my tracks. "You're not mad, right?"

"No, I'm not mad."

He didn't seem to believe me.

"Really?"

"Yes, really."

He frowned. "Aren't you going to scold me? Tell me how messed up I am or how terrible I treated you? There has to be something you want to get angry at me for."

I paused. "I can't think of anything right now, but I'll get back to you if I do."

He chuckled sadly. "I'd actually prefer it if you were mad or yelled at me."

"I think you torture yourself enough."

Parker laughed huskily, but there was nothing happy about his laughter.

"Conan being Conan," he murmured.

I watched him walk away. As his silhouette disappeared around the corner, I found myself smiling.

Conan being Conan. What beautiful words to say.

Chapter 12: My Friend Date

There was a knock at my door, and I went to open it.

"Yo, dandelion," Parker said, sliding past me and letting himself in.

"Hello, Parker." I smiled, still looking out the door frame where he once stood. Two weeks had passed since that night. We never brought it up, but ever since, Parker had been coming to my house more often. Even though he had nothing in particular to tell me, he'd stop by and hang out for an hour or two.

Parker picked up the turkey sandwich I didn't finish and took a big bite before opening the fridge.

"Are you vegetarian? There's meat in the sandwich," I asked with worry.

He snorted. "Do I look like a vegetarian?"

"I don't think vegetarians look a certain way," I murmured.

He pursed his lips, opened his mouth, then closed it. "No, I'm not vegetarian."

Parker took out a juice box and walked over to me. He placed it between my hands, ripping the plastic from the straw with his teeth and poking it into the hole. He leaned forward, and I held it for him as he took a long sip.

I didn't feel as sick as I used to whenever Parker stood close to me. Though he made a great effort not to come close, which was hard for him considering that he was a man who enjoyed physical touch. Some people expressed their feelings through words, Parker needed human contact. It was his way of showing affection.

"I got into a fight with Greg," he said. "The old geezer said he'd fix the pipes weeks ago, but it wasn't until I threatened to break his kneecaps that he came to fix them. What about you? Are you still taking cold showers?"

"Yes. I'm still waiting for Greg to come by."

"Tell him you'll break his knees if he doesn't," Parker instructed. He stopped, studied my tiny frame, then scowled. "On second thoughts, just call him."

I smiled. "I will."

Parker finished the sandwich and juice in seconds and returned to the kitchen to look for food.

"You don't eat a lot," he said, opening the empty cabinets. He swiped his finger and rubbed his index and thumb. "There's more dust than food."

"No, I don't eat a lot."

He studied me from head to toe again. "Yeah, you don't look like you do. Do you eat three meals a day?"

"I try."

Parker frowned, but before he could say anything, I spoke first.

"Do you need anything?" I asked before he interrogated me like Dr. George Phil.

"No, I came here to give you something. Catch." He tossed an object that he pulled out of his pocket, and it hit my chest and fell on the floor.

Parker blinked and grumbled, "We'll work on that," as he scooped it up and placed it in my hands. "Here, for you."

My eyes widened at the orange earplug case. "These are for me?" I asked, my voice barely above a whisper.

"Don't cry. They only cost a dollar."

"Thank you, Parker."

"I know it gets noisy at night. These might help you sleep better."

"Thank you."

"You already said that."

"I know."

Parker studied my face and sighed. "Typical dandelion," he murmured, his voice soft. "Anyway, I was wondering if you wanted to study together. You can read your philosophy books, and I'll study for my chemistry test. I'll make you another sandwich. Just give me a sec while I grab some ingredients upstairs."

"I can't today," I told him, and he stopped in his tracks, frowning.

"Are you busy?" he asked, trying to mask his disappointment.

"I'm going to the mall with Freddie."

He snorted. "The mall? What, are you two going shopping for bras and heels?"

"Freddie wants me to help him buy a present."

"For who?"

"I can't tell you."

Parker grinned, leaning against the door frame. "Now I *really* want to know," he said, mischief sparkling in his dark eyes.

"I have to leave now. Goodbye, Parker." But Parker pushed himself off the door frame and blocked my path. I stepped sideways to walk past him, but he mimicked the gesture, blocking my path again.

"You're hiding something," Parker said, a sinful grin on his face. "Does Freddie have a crush?"

"I can't tell you."

"So that's a yes." Parker's smile widened. "Redhead found himself a girlfriend? This is some juicy stuff."

I imagined Parker with devil horns and tail, plotting many evil ways to tease Freddie.

"How come he told you and not me?" Parker asked.

"You'd make fun of him."

"I wouldn't," Parker replied defensively. He paused before bursting into laughter. "Oh, who am I kidding, of course I would. Come on, let's go."

I stared at him quizzically.

"Freddie has zero experience in the dating game. Who'll give him advice on what to gift his girlfriend if not me?"

I raised my hand, and he grimaced.

"Dandelion, you're great and all, but have you ever been on a date?"

"No."

"Have you gone out with anyone?"

"No."

Parker shrugged. "Point proven. Worst-case scenario, you're going to tell Freddie to buy a philosophical book about how miserable humans are, and Freddie is going to panic and buy the most expensive thing in the mall."

Before I knew it, we were both walking down the stairs together. Parker was great at persuading people.

"I wonder what idiot fell for that idiot," Parker hummed.

"He's older than him."

He snapped his head towards me in astonishment.

"*He*? Freddie likes dudes?" he stuttered.

I clasped my hands over my mouth even though it was already too late.

"Shit, no wonder I've never seen him with a girl."

I frowned. "Please don't make fun of Freddie."

"Relax, I'm not that kind of guy."

"Can we take the bus? It's on my bucket list."

"Don't you have a car?"

"I do, but I've never taken the city bus."

"Why not?"

"Because I have a car. I've never taken the city bus before, and I'd like to make more memories with you."

Parker stopped in his steps. He was a floor below me and had to look up to meet my gaze.

"It can be a friend date," I exclaimed. "It'll be a special memory."

He frowned. "You sound like you're leaving."

"I am," I reminded him. "Next year, in July."

Parker blinked in surprise, then his lips pressed together. He ran his fingers ran through his dark hair and continued down the stairs. Maybe he didn't want to take public transportation.

"We can take my car if you'd like," I offered.

"Bus," I heard him say two floors down. "We're taking the bus."

***

We were inside the bus, sitting at the very back. The seats and windows shook with every small bump in the uneven pavement, jostling the passengers back and forth. I studied the people inside the bus. There was a curious mixture of cozy and bored individuals who seemed desperate to reach their destination. Some feigned sleep, others did crosswords, and another group read newspapers.

I enjoyed watching others. Knowing that others existed, that other people were living similarly or differently, but never equivalently, was beautiful. Everyone on this bus was experiencing every second of the same reality in their own way.

My gaze shifted towards Parker. He was handsome in a multitude of ways. He fit conventional beauty standards: masculine, strong, alluring... But I liked his eyes. They were cold and distant, but those rare moments when they softened and showed who Parker truly was were the moments I loved most.

"What?" he asked, his gaze meeting mine.

"Thank you for being my friend date," I said.

Parker looked away, resting his elbow against the window and his jaw against his knuckles. He was silent for a moment.

"Do you have to leave?" he asked, his voice suddenly quiet. "Next year, I mean. Can't you stay?"

Before I could reply, his eyes widened. "Shit, this is our stop!" he exclaimed, and Parker pulled me to my feet. The bus was about to depart, but Parker pressed the stop button.

"Sir, the door!"

"Please!" I added frantically.

The driver looked annoyed but opened the door for us, and we hopped off, laughing.

"So how was your first bus ride?"

I smiled. "I enjoyed it."

He grinned and said, "You're the only person I know who enjoys riding the bus." It wasn't until he let go of my hand to take out a cigarette that I noticed we had been holding hands the entire time. Parker didn't seem to have even noticed.

"Wait for me inside the mall. I'll join you when I'm done." He went to a stranger and asked for a lighter, and I entered the mall alone. I looked down at my hand and flexed my fingers as if I had discovered a new superpower.

For the first time in what felt like forever, someone held my hand, and I didn't feel sick.

Chapter 13: Freddie's Boyfriend

Freddie was surprised when he saw Parker beside me. I explained everything and apologized, but he shook his head, saying that Parker would have found out anyway.

"So, who's the unlucky man?" Parker asked.

Freddie told us his name was Martin, and that they had met at a bar. They'd been dating for over two months, and Freddie wanted to buy him something special to celebrate their third month together. I thought it was adorable, but Parker made a face of disgust and called him a "sentimental fool." When Freddie told Parker he could leave if he thought the idea was stupid, Parker shrugged and said he had nothing to do anyway. Deep down, I knew he cared.

We went to a perfume shop, and Parker helped Freddie pick a cologne.

"Here, smell this. It's the best one they have," Parker assured, spraying cologne onto a small piece of paper and fanning it before handing it to Freddie.

He sniffed it, and his nose wrinkled. "It smells like you."

"Because it's the one I use." Parker laughed, which explained what he had said prior.

"No offense, but I don't want to date someone who smells like you."

"None taken, Chucky. You're not my type either." Parker turned towards me. "Dandelion, c'mere."

I did, and Parker twirled his finger in a circular motion. "Spin for me."

I waddled in place like a penguin while turning around, and Parker sprayed the cologne over me. He leaned in and sniffed the air.

"Yup. Smell's just like me. You are now officially Parker property."

Freddie frowned. "You can't claim Conan as yours."

"Excuse you, he's my friend date. You're the one who's butting in." His eyes shifted towards me, and he winked. "Ain't that right, dandelion?"

He and Freddie continued to test the different scents, but the smell was so strong that my nose hurt. I told them I'd wait for them outside. I crouched down and rested my chin on my knees. My clothes smelled like Parker, and I liked that they did.

My phone rang. It was Dr. Philip George.

"Hello, Dr. Philip George. How are you?"

"I'm doing great, thank you. I hope you're doing well, Conan."

"Yes, I am. I'm shopping with my friends."

"Shopping? With friends?" He sounded shocked. I wondered if the connection was bad.

"Yes, doctor, shopping with friends," I repeated.

"That's fantastic! I'm glad you're going out and meeting new people. Good for you, Conan. I'm so proud." I could hear him scribbling notes.

"Have you been taking your meds?" he asked, returning to his usual routine of questions.

"No, I haven't."

"Why not?"

"Because the Dark Thoughts haven't been bothering me. I don't think I'm sick anymore," I said, hopeful.

"Conan, what you have doesn't disappear in a day. I know you want to get better, but you never know when the Dark Thoughts will return. Have you been eating?"

"No, not much," I admitted.

"You see? If you don't take your meds, your appetite will keep dropping, and you won't eat. You can't lose any more weight."

"Yes, doctor, I know," I murmured, tracing a circle on my knee.

"Have you found a local doctor?"

"No."

I felt like my answers kept disappointing him.

He sighed. "I'm going to contact a doctor I know and schedule a medical checkup for you. I'll send you the date and time, and I want you to be there, alright?"

I didn't answer.

"Alright?" he asked again.

"Alright," I replied quietly. I wanted to hang up.

"I'll call you again in a few days to see how you're doing. Don't forget your meds, okay?"

"Goodbye."

My chest hurt, and I didn't have the heart to say his name. I hung up before he answered and let out a quiet sigh.

"You're going to deflate like a balloon if you sigh like that," someone said. I looked up and saw Parker standing in front of me. I stood up, but I got up so quickly I became light-headed. Black spots darkened my vision, and I felt myself crouch back down, but Parker caught my arm.

"Hey, I didn't literally mean to deflate like a balloon." He laughed worriedly.

"Where is Freddie?"

"He's at the cashier. He'll be out soon."

"I'm tired," I whispered. Parker helped me sit down on nearby benches, and my head fell on his strong shoulder.

"You're probably low on sugar. Did you eat anything before coming out?"

"No," I whispered, closing my eyes.

"I'll go buy you something sugary," he said, but I held onto his arm, shaking my head.

"Please don't go," I murmured. "Will you stay with me?"

There was a long pause, and I wondered if I was dreaming.

"Yeah, of course," he finally said.

"Am I going to die?"

I felt his muscles stiffen at the question.

"No, Conan, it's normal for your blood pressure to drop when you stand up too quickly. Orthostatic hypotension is common."

"Orthostatic hippopotamus?"

Parker laughed, shaking his head. "Orthostatic hypotension," he repeated. "It's when blood pools in your legs. It takes your body a moment to squeeze blood out of the large veins in your legs and rev up your heart."

"You're very smart."

"I'm a bio-chem major."

"I feel like someone is draining the life out of me," I told him. "I once lost consciousness and bumped my head when I fell. I woke up in a pool of blood and Dr. Philip George was very upset."

"You see a doctor?" He sounded concerned. I didn't want Parker to see me as a broken, sick man. Maybe if I remained silent, he would let it slide. But he didn't.

"If you need a medical checkup, I can ask my dad to give you one for free. His clinic isn't too far from here."

I shook my head. "I get dizzy sometimes, that's all."

There was a pause.

"Dandelion, you know you can tell me anything, right?"

If only I could speak as freely as I wrote, then perhaps communicating with Parker would be much easier. But I was too tired to arrange my thoughts. I must have fallen asleep because I was in a moving vehicle when I woke up. I opened my eyes and saw that I was sitting in the backseat of Freddie's car. There was a sandwich and a juice box beside me. Freddie was driving, and Parker sat in the passenger's seat.

"You've been acting normal," Freddie said to Parker.

"Is that your way of complimenting me?"

"You haven't been sleeping around as much these past few days, and you don't come home drunk anymore," Freddie went on.

"I'm fulfilling my new year's resolution to live a clean and sober life."

"New years was ten months ago."

"Better late than sorry."

"So it has nothing to do with Conan?"

There was a pause. "What do you mean?"

"You smoke less, drink and party less, and see fewer girls. You're becoming the Parker I knew before your anger issues and addictions. You've changed since Conan arrived," Freddie said softly.

"He's a good friend."

"He is, so stop lashing out at him whenever you're having another one of your outbursts."

"It's hard for me to control my emotions. I don't mean what I say."

"I know," Freddie replied. He sounded sad.

"Anyway, tell me about your secret boyfriend," Parker said, quickly changing the subject.

Freddie snorted and asked, "Why do you care?", but his voice wasn't harsh.

Parker snorted too. "To make sure you're not dating trash."

"He's the son of a very famous entrepreneur."

"So he's rich trash."

Freddie must have punched Parker, who yelped.

"Hey!" he snapped.

"He's a decent guy," Freddie said.

"He better be."

There was a long pause.

"You know I'm happy for you, right?" Parker said after a moment of silence.

"Yeah, I know," Freddie replied. My eyes were closed, but I knew he was smiling.

Chapter 14: Sir Anderson

I made a greater effort to eat my fruits and vegetables. I didn't want Parker and Freddie to worry. After Parker found out that I had orthostatic hypotension, he came to my house once a week with bags of food.

He filled my cupboards with pasta and grains and supplied my refrigerator with fruits and vegetables. Every time I asked him how much he spent on groceries so I could pay him back, but he wouldn't tell me.

Parker and Freddie would also take me out to eat on Saturday nights, showing me their favorite restaurants and riding the bus with me. Everything was fine until Dr. George Philip sent me a message informing me of the date and address for my medical checkup. As reluctant as I was, I knew I couldn't disobey him, so I typed the location into my GPS and headed out.

I arrived at a private clinic, checked in, and met with the doctor. He was a tall man with dark hair and eyes. His handsomeness struck me. Even at his age, which I assumed was in his late forties, he aged like fine wine: a clean-shaven jaw, sharp cheekbones, thick groomed brows...

I walked into his office, and we went through the usual medical protocol. I couldn't help but stare at him when he took down notes. He looked familiar, but I couldn't put my finger on a name. Perhaps we had met in another life.

"Your heart seems to beat at a normal rate," he said, removing the blood pressure cuff from my arm. "Have you had any other problems apart from the dizziness?"

"No, sir."

I knew I should have addressed him as a "doctor," but I felt like "sir" suited him better.

"Dr. Philip informed me you had problems eating. Have you been working on that?"

"I've been trying."

"We'll check the scale. You'll need to take off your clothes."

My heart pulsed rapidly, and I felt goosebumps crawl onto my skin. My eyes dropped from his merciless dark eyes, and I stared at my lap. My jeans looked bigger. Or perhaps I became thinner.

"Can I keep my clothes on?" I asked quietly.

"I'm afraid not. I need to write down your exact weight."

"I can weigh myself and tell you the number," I suggested.

His voice remained indifferent. "We have patients who lie about their weight."

I frowned, starting to panic. "I promise I won't lie." I wanted to leave this clinic and never come back. I wished I could sew my clothes into my skin so they'd never come off.

"I believe you." His husky voice softened, and I looked up at him. "But as a doctor, I need to follow the rules, or I wouldn't be a doctor, would I?"

"You would, just not a good one."

A smile grew on Dr. Anderson's lips, and he looked even more handsome. I wondered if the men and women in this clinic ever got distracted working with him. They probably did. I tried negotiating with Dr. Anderson, but he was firm with the rules. Unfortunately, he was a good doctor.

We went to a room with lots of medical supplies. I took my clothes off but kept my briefs on. Dr. Anderson showed no interest in my body and remained professional the entire time. I mounted on the scale, gulping air, hoping it would increase the number, and Dr. Anderson wrote the results.

"Thank you, Conan. I'll wait for you in the other room while you dress." He left and closed the door behind him. I put my clothes back on and joined him in his office. I realized my hands were shaking. How long had I been trembling? My legs wouldn't stop either.

"How are the results?" My throat was dry.

"You're underweight," he said. "According to the medical files Dr. Philip sent me, you've lost two kilograms since your last medical checkup."

"I walk a lot."

"You don't eat enough," he corrected.

I squeezed my hands together tightly, which only worsened the shaking.

"But I'm trying," I insisted gently. "A very good friend of mine has filled my cupboards with food, and he takes me out to eat when he's not busy."

"He sounds like a very good friend."

"He's a very good person, too." Thinking and speaking of Parker calmed me, and my body seemed to tremble a little less. A warm feeling spread inside my chest as I thought of Parker's wonderful forehead and scowl.

"Make sure to thank that person."

"I will," I said, taking a mental note.

Dr. Anderson asked me a couple more questions and took down notes as he did. I wondered if he'd tell Dr. George Philip everything. I hoped he wouldn't.

"I'm going to write lists of food you need to eat daily. If you want to get better, you'll follow the regimen dutifully. Doctors can only do so much for their patients. The rest is up to you."

I felt like a heavy bag of burdens had just been thrown onto my frail shoulders.

"You want to get better, don't you?" He stared at me with his piercing eyes, and I gulped. I nodded, but only because he scared me.

He began typing into his computer and printed a paper, handing it to me. It was a schedule with snacks and meals I had to eat every day, and it looked more like a challenge than a cure.

"This is a lot of food."

"Humans need to eat to live. Don't you ever get hungry?"

"No, not anymore." I paused. "Does that mean I'm not human?"

Dr. Anderson chuckled. His laugh was deep and soft, like gentle ripples in a calm lake. It could be someone's ringtone.

"Rest assured, you are very much human."

That didn't reassure me one bit, but I nodded.

"Thank you."

"Your lack of hunger is most likely due to what happened to you in the past, but that doesn't mean you aren't human, Conan. Never forget that."

"Yes, sir."

"I know it won't be easy, but you must keep trying. You're a smart boy and better than what you give yourself credit for."

"That's very kind of you, but you don't know me."

"I know what happened to you," he said grimly. I felt ashamed and embarrassed and couldn't look him in the eyes anymore.

"Come again soon, okay? I'll schedule our next appointment." Dr. Anderson asked me which day I could come, and I told him in two weeks. I gathered my papers and stood up. Dr. Anderson opened the door for me, but my eyes widened when Parker stood outside the doorframe. He was just about to knock.

"Dandelion?" he asked, his eyebrows shooting up in surprise. I felt the blood in my face drain down my neck. My stomach curled, and my chest tightened. I felt like I was having another orthostatic hippopotamus. "What are you doing here?"

Before I could say anything, Dr. Anderson spoke. "Son, you're early. I told you to come at three."

And then everything made sense. The dark hair and eyes, the height, the similar jawline... Dr. Anderson and I hadn't met in a previous lifetime. He was Parker's father.

***

Dear,

Parker Anderson is mad at me.

It's been a week since we bumped into each other at his father's clinic.

I can still remember that day as if it were yesterday. He pulled me aside and bombarded me with questions: Are you okay? Why are you here? Are you sick? Why didn't you tell me? Did you lie to me? I remained silent, not knowing how to respond. He raised his voice, frustrated, confused, and worried. He had every right to be upset. Yet, I couldn't answer a single one of his questions.

Dr. Anderson, his father, stepped in and told me to go home, which upset Parker. As I left, I could hear Parker arguing with his father. He then shouted my name, but I didn't stop or look back and left as quickly as I could.

Did Dr. Anderson tell Parker about my problems? I hope he didn't. He is a doctor; it's against the law to give confidential information. I've been avoiding Parker at all costs, and now, I think he's the one avoiding me.

Whenever I see Parker at school, he's with a girl. He's been inviting them to his place, and I hear them laughing and pleasure fighting. Most of the time, he sounds drunk, and that saddens me deeply. He is returning to his bad habits, but so am I. It's been three days since I haven't had a full meal. The Dark Thoughts have returned. I try to busy myself with books and philosophy, but nothing works. I wish I could apologize to Parker, but I don't know if he'll forgive me.

I'm a terrible friend.

It hurts.

Yours truly

Chapter 15: Sleepover

Freddie and I were chatting on the front steps of our apartment complex. He was telling me stories about him and his boyfriend. I tried to listen, but I couldn't focus. My mind kept drifting to Parker, wondering what he was doing, how he was, and if we were still friends.

"...and then a kangaroo punched me in the face."

"Oh, how wonderful," I murmured absently.

Freddie frowned, waving his hand in front of my face. "Conan, you're spacing out."

"I'm sorry, I have a lot on my mind."

Freddie nibbled his lip, studying my face. "Parker?"

I nodded. "Parker."

"It's been two weeks. You two still aren't talking?"

I shook my head, wanting to cry. "I'm a terrible friend."

"Hey, don't say that. You, out of all people, shouldn't be saying that. You're an amazing friend," he argued. "Friendships have their ups and downs, that's all. Do you want to talk about what happened?"

I told Freddie how I bumped into Parker at his father's clinic and how upset he was that I didn't tell him about my problems. Well, I told him, I just didn't tell him how bad they were.

"The books never said that giving medical background was required to stay friends."

"Which books?"

"The books that help me understand human behavior. When I was young, the doctors told me I was special. I think it was their nice way of saying I was different. They said I would have a hard time socializing and understanding other people. So I read books to help me understand."

"Every human is unique, Conan. Books give us ideas and concepts, but there are exceptions in reality, and Parker seems to be one of them. Humans aren't objects you put into boxes. You have to learn to adapt to each individual."

"I don't know how to do that."

Freddie smiled gently. "Communication."

I stared at my fingers and pressed them together.

"I know it's not easy talking about your problems. Even though you've never told me, I know you struggle," he said, his eyebrows creasing slightly. "Parker has a hard time expressing his feelings too. He doesn't get close to many people, but he gives them his everything when he does. If he's mad at you, it's because he cares, and if he isn't talking to you, it's because he doesn't know how to convey his feelings without throwing a tantrum. He's being cautious."

Silence hung over our shoulders, and I took a moment to gather my thoughts and rearrange them into constructive sentences to communicate my thoughts to Freddie.

"I'd like to tell you and Parker about my problems one day. I can't right now, but I will when I'm ready."

Freddie reached out and put his hand over mine. A shiver crawled down my spine, but I didn't feel sick enough to pull away. Or rather, I fought back the urge to pull away.

"Take your time. We'll wait as long as you need," he assured, giving me a gentle squeeze. "Parker too. He'll wait."

"I don't think he likes me anymore."

Freddie chuckled, shaking his head. "I think it's the exact opposite. He cares about you more than he shows."

"How do you know?"

"His eyes shine the brightest when he looks at you."

I blinked blankly. "But his eyes are black," I said in a matter-of-fact tone.

Freddie smiled. "Exactly."

The door opened behind us, and Parker stepped out of the building. My chest tightened with excitement and pain.

"Hey, redhead," Parker said.

"Hey, addict," Freddie replied.

He didn't spare me a glance.

I smiled with a wave as I said, "Hello, Parker," but Parker ignored me and walked down the stairs, leaving an aroma of alcohol behind him. He was drunk. My stomach twisted into a nervous knot.

Freddie frowned. "You can at least say hi to Conan."

Parker laughed dryly. "I can also raise a fundraiser and donate my organs."

"Are you really going to be that petty? Conan did nothing wrong. If he's not ready to talk, then he's not ready."

"Quit playing the knight in shining armor. He has a mouth of his own. Maybe it's time he puts it to use."

I flinched at his harsh words, squeezing my hands tightly together. I could see regret flash through Parker's eyes, but he quickly concealed it with a scowl.

"Why didn't you tell us you were sick?" he growled.

"I did tell you."

"You didn't tell us you were sick to the point where you had to see a doctor!" Parker raised his voice, trying his best not to slur his words.

"I didn't think it was important."

Parker's dark eyes flared with anger. "Of course, it's important!" He ran a frustrated hand through his tousled hair, clenching his jaw. Then his voice went quiet. "It's you we're talking about. Of course, it's important."

My throat constricted at his words. Parker ran the flat of his palm over his face. His eyes looked darker and emptier, and I wondered why he looked so miserable.

"Do you know how shitty it felt finding out that you were sick through my dad?"

"Did he tell you?" I asked in horror.

Parker narrowed his eyes. "No, he didn't. He'd dig his own grave before breaking the rules, but it doesn't take a genius to put two and two together. He treats specific patients that—"

I closed my eyes and covered my ears, refusing to hear it. It felt like Parker was stripping me bare naked and exposing me to the world, and I thought it was very cruel of him.

"What's wrong with you?" I heard Freddie yell at Parker. They began to argue, raising their voices and shouting at each other. Parker moved his hand angrily when he yelled, which was when I noticed that he was holding his motorcycle keys. Was he planning on driving drunk?

"You're messed up, you know that?" Freddie hissed.

"Tell me something I don't know," Parker sneered. "Whatever, I'm leaving."

"No!" I blurted. They turned towards me, their eyes widening in shock.

"Are you crying?" Parker stuttered, his anger vanishing in a heartbeat. I raised my fingers to touch my face and realized that I was. I tried to wipe the tears away, but they kept dribbling off my chin.

"Great job, Fred, you made dandelion cry," Parker mumbled. "Now we're both jerks. Just so you know, it feels shitty being in the same category as you. Why can't you be more decent than me? I'm supposed to be the fuck up, not you."

Freddie's jaw dropped to the ground.

"It's not Freddie's fault. You promised you wouldn't drive drunk."

Parker shifted his gaze, licking his lips. "Stop crying, dandelion."

Rather than a demand, it sounded more like a plea. Parker raised my chin, wiping away my tears with his rough hands.

"Don't make that face. I'm sorry, okay? I won't go."

"I don't believe you." And I didn't. Not when he broke the first promise he made. Parker gave me his motorcycle keys, and I closed my fingers around them.

"I won't go," he whispered again. "Come on, don't cry. Look at me."

I tried to look at him, but all I could see were tears. I tried squinting my eyes.

"You're blurry," I finally said.

"How about you two talk things out later?" Freddie suggested. "We'll let Conan calm down while you sober up."

Parker let go of my hand, his face filled with guilt. "Right."

"How about we watch a movie at my place? We can make snacks and watch a movie," Freddie said, trying to lighten the mood.

"Like a sleepover?" I asked, rubbing my eyes.

"Yeah, like a sleepover. And since Parker is so obsessed with you, he's invited too. But only if you want him there."

"I do," I murmured.

Parker shoved his hands into his pockets. I thought he would refuse, but "Cool," was all he said.

Freddie turned towards him with hardened eyes. "But you're invited once you sober up."

Parker shrugged. "Fine."

"Can I invite Zev?" I asked.

"That's a great idea!" Freddie beamed. "We can head upstairs and get the snacks ready."

I nodded, and Parker was about to follow, but Freddie glared at him.

"Sober up, Parker, I'm serious."

"I just want to talk to Conan privately," he murmured.

"You can talk to Conan later," Freddie said.

Before Parker could protest, Freddie's voice softened. "You'll regret it a lot less, Parker, trust me. You and I both know you talk shit when you're drunk."

He scowled. "I'm not drunk,"

"You're drunk," I said.

"Thanks for the support, dandelion."

"You're welcome."

He stared at me, then sighed. "Typical dandelion," he whispered, but the tip of his lips curved to a small smile.

I didn't know why I felt so relieved hearing a name that didn't belong to me. Freddie and I went upstairs while Parker stayed outside to cool his head. I took my pajamas and toothbrush and went upstairs to join Freddie.

It was getting dark, and Freddie told me to close the windows before the mosquitoes came in. I went to the kitchen windows and saw Parker standing outside the building. He looked much smaller from up here and was smoking a cigarette, looking straight ahead without any particular expression on his face. When I closed the windows, I couldn't help but think how lonely he looked.

Chapter 16: Movie Night

"Guess who brought candy?" Zev sang when I opened the door for him. He raised a bag full of colorful candy, and I smiled so widely that my face hurt. Zev's smile was contagious, and his presence could lift even the most burdened hearts.

"You did!" I exclaimed.

"You bet I did." He winked, putting a toffee-flavored candy in my hand. We both unwrapped our toffees and popped them into our mouths, which had become our greeting ritual. Freddie and Parker came out of the living room to greet Zev.

"Ah, the famous Parker and the cute boy with freckles! I've heard so much about you two," Zev said, shaking their hands. "It's an honor."

Freddie smiled. "You must be Zev. We have international law together, right? I loved the presentation you gave last week on European human rights."

"I'm glad you did. It took me way too much time to do the research."

"Well, it was worth it. You were brilliant."

Parker gagged. "If you two lovebirds are finished flirting, let's get this sleepover over with," he grumbled, taking my arm and pulling me to the living room.

Freddie sighed. "I have a boyfriend."

Zev chuckled. "And I have a girlfriend."

Parker snorted with an eye roll. "How tragic for you both." He sat on the couch and sprawled his legs out. I sat on the floor below him, hugging my knees to my chest. Parker asked me if I wanted to sit beside him, but I shook my head, saying that I preferred the floor. Freddie and Zev shared the couch. They started to chat, and I reached out to grab the bottle of apple juice on the coffee table.

Parker took the bottle from my hand and cracked the lid open for me, pouring me a cup and putting a metal straw in before handing it to me.

"Thank you," I said with a smile. He ignored me.

"So, what movie do you guys want to watch?" Freddie asked.

"I say we watch a horror movie," Parker grunted.

Freddie frowned. "I hate horror movies."

Parker grinned. "Which is why we should watch one."

"Can we watch Stuart Little?" I asked, sipping my juice.

Parker grimaced. "The movie with the talking rat?"

"That's Ratatouille," Freddie replied.

"I don't think the rat spoke in Ratatouille," Zev said, rubbing his jaw.

"Not to the humans, but to the other rats it did," Freddie retorted.

"Well, duh, how else are rats supposed to communicate?" Parker snorted, and slowly, our conversation digressed.

We spent an hour debating on Ratatouille before arguing about what movie we'd watch. Freddie wanted to watch a crime movie, Zev suggested we watch a comedy, and Parker insisted on a horror movie. When they asked me what I wanted to watch, I said I didn't mind as long as we watched it together. We couldn't decide, and Parker was running out of popcorn to throw at Freddie, so we solved the matter by playing a round of rock, paper, scissors.

"Winner gets to choose which movie we watch," Parker said, his dark eyes glistening with determination as he pulled up his sleeves, revealing his muscles and the veins that stretched in between. "Losers get flicked on the forehead."

"Won't that hurt?" I asked, putting a hand over my forehead as if a ghost had flicked me.

Parker rolled his eyes. "That's the point."

"What's the point?" I asked, clueless.

Parker opened his mouth, then closed it. "Who raised this child?" he asked, jerking a thumb at me.

"Alright, let's play," Zev said, cracking his knuckles.

Parker smirked. "I hope you guys are ready to lose."

Despite Parker's desire to inflict pain on his friends, I thought it was cute how his voice quickened when he was excited and how he smiled like an excited child. His eyes met mine, and I felt butterflies tickle my stomach and quickly averted my gaze. Why did I avert my gaze?

We all shouted in unison, "Rock, paper, scissors!"

Parker played scissors, Freddie and I played paper, and Zev played rock. We repeated a few more rounds until Parker, Zev, and I played paper while Freddie played rock.

"I'm always the first to lose," Freddie groaned.

Parker seemed too excited to flick him. He pushed Freddie's bangs away, and I flinched when I heard the impact of the flick.

Freddie howled in pain, rubbing his sore forehead. "Ouch!"

"That's on you, loser." Parker shrugged, looking happy and smug.

Freddie narrowed his eyes before turning towards Zev who was flexing his fingers. Freddie frowned with a gulp. "Hey Zev, you'll go easy on me, right?"

"Sorry, Fred." He smiled apologetically, flicking Freddie, who hissed in pain.

Parker and Zev high-fived, and Freddie sulked, the skin on his forehead turning the same color as his hair. I got up and tried to flick Freddie but accidentally flicked the strands of his bangs instead.

"Oh, I'm sorry, I missed."

"Dandelion, you just missed a lifetime opportunity!" Parker cried.

"Can I try again?" I asked. Before Parker could scream yes, Zev came to Freddie's rescue and lowered Freddie's bangs, gently rearranging his hair.

"I think Fred's gone through enough pain," he said with a chuckle.

"Don't act innocent," Freddie grumbled, pushing Zev's hand away.

"Alright, next match," Parker said. "You guys, dandelion?"

"Ye—"

"ROCK, PAPER, SCISSORS!" he screamed.

Zev lost, and Parker and I both flicked him. The "clack" sound when Parker flicked him made me cringe. While Zev howled in pain, Freddie was on the floor, dying from laughter.

Parker had the proudest smile on his face, as if he had just won the Oscars. I looked at each one of my friends and smiled. Little moments like these were precious.

We often remember the big events that happened in our lives, but the most mundane ones were the ones that truly made us happy. The ones where we felt like nothing was happening. The forgettable ones.

It was my turn to flick Zev, but Parker quickly stopped me. "You're not missing this one-in-a-lifetime opportunity again. It's all in the middle finger."

"The middle finger?"

"Like this," he said, rearranging my fingers for me. "Press the tip of your middle finger against your thumb and then release."

I did as he said and didn't miss. Parker was proud of me, and that strange feeling in my chest returned. It felt like a boa was constricting my lungs, suffocating me. But I didn't hate the feeling. Was I a masochist? I'd have to discuss this with my therapist next week.

"It's just you and me, dandelion." Parker grinned. "Rock, paper, scissors!"

I looked down and realized that I had lost. Parker didn't seem as excited as I thought he would be. I pushed my bangs away and turned towards him.

"Go easy on him," Freddie said worriedly when Parker rolled his wrists and flexed his fingers in preparation.

"He'll fly across the room if you flick him too hard," Zev warned him.

"I can't wait," Freddie moaned, putting a hand over his eyes.

"Dandelion can handle it. He can handle anything, ain't that right?" Parker said, his gaze meeting mine. And despite losing, I felt like a winner. Parker scooted closer towards me, and I looked at him. We hadn't sat so close to each other since our bus ride to the mall.

"You ready?" he asked.

"I don't think anyone is ready for pain."

"Close your eyes. It'll be over in a sec."

I closed my eyes and waited for the pain. I felt a gentle gust of air instead.

"I missed," Parker murmured.

My eyes fluttered open as Freddie gasped.

"You never miss."

"There's a first for everything," he grumbled.

Freddie and Zev shared a look, and a broad smile spread across their faces, as if a secret message had passed through them. They began nudging each other, giggling like giddy girls.

Parker grabbed the closest cushion and threw it at them. The two of them burst into laughter despite getting hit in the face.

"I'll give you another chance," I told Parker, worried that he was upset, but he had already gotten up and was heading to the front of the room where the DVD folder was.

He chose a horror movie.

Chapter 17: Homophobic

When I woke up, the TV was turned off, and someone had cleaned the snacks. Someone had draped a blanket over my shoulders. Gentle snores filled the air, and I turned to its source. Zev and Freddie were snuggled next to each other, sound asleep. I slowly picked myself off the ground and wrapped my blanket around them. I hope they didn't mind sharing. Zev snored, and Freddie's mouth hung open as he slept. I took a picture of them and smiled.

For memories.

I then tiptoed out of the living room. The wooden floor creaked under my weight. A figure sat on the window ledge inside Freddie's room. Day or night, Parker's silhouette always seemed lonely. A cold autumn breeze came through the windows, and I shivered.

Maybe it's best if I leave him alone.

But when I stepped back, the wooden floor creaked loudly, and Parker glanced over his shoulder. His eyes met mine, and my heart fluttered, then constricted.

Why am I so nervous? My hands feel clammier than usual.

"Good evening, Parker. I didn't mean to bother you."

"You haven't said anything."

"Yes, I guess so," I said pensively. "But now I have."

I was about to leave when he said my name. Well, my nickname.

"Dandelion, come here," he ordered gently, his voice low and husky. I counted up to five before joining him at the window, sitting across from him. The street outside was dark, and a stray cat ran down the parking lot.

"Why are you sitting here?" I asked.

"I couldn't sleep."

Parker took a drag from his cigarette, looking outside the window. Although, there wasn't much to look at.

"Parker?"

"Mhm?"

"Why do you call me dandelion?"

"Because it rhymes with Conan."

I silently mouthed the two words to find the rhyme.

"It doesn't," I informed him.

Parker flinched and grumbled, "It almost does." After a long pause, he said, "You remind me of dandelions."
He looked at me, and a nervous pang shot through me. I could feel my heart thump against my thin chest, which almost hurt. A mix of fear, disgust, and excitement rushed through me. When Parker looked at me, he reminded me I existed, and I thought it was a terrible power to give someone.

I pulled my knees to my chest for comfort, wondering when he'd look away from me. But strangely, part of me didn't want him to look elsewhere.

"You scare me," Parker whispered, letting the cigarette burn between his fingers. "I feel like if I close my eyes and let you out of my sight for even a second, the wind will take you away, and you'll become a million particles drifting in the air. That's what dandelions do, don't they? You make a wish, and they vanish."

My eyes widened in surprise.

"I'm sorry for not controlling my anger. I panic whenever someone I care about deteriorates. I've already lost so many people, the thought of losing any more... It doesn't sit well with me."

Parker must have read the confused expression on my face because he said, "My mom died giving birth to me."

There was a pause.

He smirked. "Aren't you gonna say you're sorry for her death?"

"I don't think I should apologize for a natural phenomenon. People don't apologize for water being clear or air containing oxygen."

Parker blinked, then smiled. "You're right. I always hate it when people apologize for her death. There's nothing to be sorry about. I never knew her, so I don't feel as sad as I would if I had known her."

I nodded. "That's very optimistic of you."

He laughed softly. "Though, I do feel guilty."

"Why?"

"Even though I didn't know her, my dad did. She gave her life for me, but I'm not exactly the ideal son they dreamt of, yet I'm here. Alive." His dark eyes were unfocused, and his voice was distant. "My dad probably regrets having me, and he probably wishes it were his wife that lived and not me."

He let out a quiet sigh. "No, I know that if my dad had the choice, he would have chosen her."

I could see guilt in Parker's eyes. He blamed himself for something that wasn't his fault.

"I don't think that's true. Your dad would do anything for you."

He raised his brows.

"Your dad loves you very much," I murmured. "Even though he doesn't say it, he loves you more than you'll ever know."

"What about you? Are your parents still alive?" he asked.

"Yes, they're still alive."

"What do they do?"

"My mother works as a nurse, and my father is a real estate agent."

Parker raised his brows with a whistle. "You must be rich. How come you settled for this cheap building? You could have lived somewhere better."

"The same reason you and Freddie chose to stay here."

"Which is?"

I smiled shyly. "I don't know."

And I didn't. Parker's father was a successful doctor, and Freddie's mother was a well-known lawyer. Their parents could have easily helped their children afford a bigger, cleaner, and overall better apartment to live in. Yet, despite having the means, the three of us chose this place. The "crappy" building. Greg's building. The one with dirty walls, a broken elevator, and busted pipes. Maybe we didn't want to feel guilty using money that wasn't ours.

Or perhaps the three of us saw a certain charm in this broken-down apartment.

Or perhaps Parker and Freddie, no matter how much they pretended to despise each other, found comfort and safety in each other's proximity. They bickered like brothers and treated each other like family. It was the purest form of friendship one could find, a family bond.

This old building compensated for its flaws by keeping us together. I didn't know why I chose this building, but I knew my reason for staying.

"I don't think your parents regret having you," I murmured.

"Why?"

"Because you're a good person."

Parker reached out and gently brushed my bangs away from my face, and I gulped. It was a bold and intimate gesture. I never enjoyed intimacy. It terrified me. The idea of being connected to someone scared me. Maybe his touch was nothing but a simple gesture of friendship, but deep down, it felt stronger.

"You think so?" he whispered, his voice soft and deep. He had a masculine smell mixed with tobacco and a hint of pine. His face was so close to mine that if he moved any closer, our lips would touch.

Parker looked deeply into my eyes, and I felt as if he was reading all my secrets, and it terrified and excited me. I couldn't help but think how tragic and beautiful this all was.

Mothered or motherless, drunk or sober, cigarettes or not, all these elements that ornamented his life were details that merely decorated his existence. But they weren't his existence itself. Nothing could change the essence of Parker's nature. It had been pre-determined the day he was created and determined the day he was born.

It was like clothes. Wearing a dress didn't make you a woman, nor did wearing a suit make you a man. External elements didn't alter one's being. Parker could drink, smoke, and have sex, but he'd still be him—and as an individual, Parker as Parker, Parker as a person, he was, in my eyes, a good man.

My chest tightened when Parker came closer to me. He was beautiful despite the shadows that stained the skin under his eyes. His dark eyes pierced through me, and I found it harder to breathe. Parker reached out, and I flinched but didn't pull away. He gently brushed away the bangs from my forehead. Normally, I'd feel sick or run away, but right now, I felt strangely nervous but brave. His warmth felt so familiar.

"You think I'm a good person," he whispered, and the corner of his lips curved into a small smile as he looked at me with a smile that didn't reach his eyes. "If you keep saying things like that, I might fall in love again."

My heart stopped, and my eyes widened.

"I'm always thinking about you. When I wake up, when I smoke, when I'm in class, when I have sex," he drawled, his husky voice sending chills down my spine. Parker was so close I could feel the warmth of his body radiate against mine.

"You're weird, you hate being touched, you keep secrets, you're impossible to understand, and you scare me in so many ways, so why does my mind keep coming back to you?"

Parker didn't seem angry. He was frustrated and confused, desperate for answers. But I didn't want to hurt Parker. Getting close to someone who'd be gone in a year would break him.

"Conan," he murmured, and when he said my name, a jolt of warmth spread through my body. If he had kissed me, I would have let him. I'd probably puke afterward, but I'd still let him. I needed to stop this before he got too attached. Before I hurt him.

"You don't know me," I blurted.

"Then tell me about yourself," he said softly.

"You'll be disappointed."

"I won't," he answered in a heartbeat.

"You'll hate me."

He wanted to know who I was, but even I didn't know. There were a million different fragments of me, and I couldn't tell which one was real. I dug my nails into my palms, feeling an overwhelming sadness wash through me as I sat there, caught between Parker and my past. Maybe that was the real Conan. The broken one.

He was about to say something, but I spoke first.

"I'm homophobic," I rasped.

I immediately regretted telling him the truth when I saw the pain flash through his dark eyes; and I knew nothing would ever be the same again.

Chapter 18: The Winter Play

Dear,

"Let's not see each other anymore."

Those were Parker's last words before he stormed out of the room and left Freddie's apartment.

I couldn't remember anything else. I couldn't remember how I fell asleep, if I fell asleep, when I woke up, how I left Freddie's apartment... But I couldn't forget the look Parker had on his face. The memory was seared into my mind, and I knew it would haunt me forever.

When he said those words, I felt my heart drop to my stomach. Life had killed me twice. This was the second time.

Yours Truly

***

Dear,

The Dark Thoughts have come back. They haunt me day and night, and I wake up crying and shaking. I've taken the stronger pills Dr. George Philip had prescribed me. We call them the "Emergency Pills" — for my worst days. It still hurts.

It's one thing to feel lonely when you're alone, but it's more terrifying when someone who was once by your side is gone. It made me understand Parker's pain and suffering and why he relied on toxic substances to fill the holes in his heart.

He hasn't spoken to me since the night of our sleepover. After I told him I was homophobic, nothing has been the same, and I doubt it ever will be. He deserved to know. But I wish he knew that the way I am isn't my fault... It isn't...

I miss Parker. I wish he'd look at me. I wish he'd talk to me. I wish he could remind me once again that I existed for other reasons than simply breathing.

Yours truly

***

Freddie had to rush to his next class when we arrived at school. He said to call me at twelve, so we could have lunch together. I smiled and waved at him, watching him jog towards the law amphitheater. I didn't have any morning classes today, but I came here because I didn't want to break the tradition of going to school with Freddie. I went to the library, smiling at those who walked past me. Most of them didn't notice, but that was okay. I was about to enter the library, but something caught my eye. I backtracked and looked at the large poster on the wall that read: *"Bergson University Theatre Club: Romeo, oh, Romeo!"*

I continued reading.

"This year, in December, the Bergson University Theatre will perform an LGBTQIA+ play directed and acted by the students themselves! It will adapt 'Romeo and Juliet,' starring two male lovers instead of your conventional heterosexual couple. Break the norms, as Shakespeare once said! (Did he? Probably not)."

I found myself giggling.

"We're looking for actors, artists, extras, and many more! Want to be the next Romeo and Clark? Sing up now! Auditions begin soon!

P.S: All the money we collect will be donated to a local organization that fights for LGBTTQQIAAP rights.

P.P.S: Our male leads don't need to be queer. Heterosexuals are welcome to play the leading actors. Remember people, this is acting! To be or not to be, that is not the question."

I smiled widely.

"Are you thinking of signing up too?" someone asked. Startled, I spun around, surprised to see a giant standing behind me. Uncomfortable with the approximation, I took a step back. He mimicked my movement, raising his hands to show he meant no harm.

"Sorry, I didn't mean to scare you." He chuckled softly, pushing back the golden curls that fell over his forehead. What a wonderful forehead.

He looked like someone who came right out of Greek mythology. He had a nicely carved jaw and a strong, tall nose. His defined features complemented his powerful body. The only unintimidating features were his bright blue eyes and charming smile. Oh, and the two dimples on his cheeks.

"Hello, mister. My name is Conan," I waved.

"Mister?" he asked, his laughter laced with amusement and confusion. "Do I look that old?"

"No, you look handsome."

He blinked before laughing again. My stomach twisted into a nervous knot.

Did I say something wrong?

"I like the honesty. Thank you, Conan."

"Thank you for remembering my name."

"I'm Ryan, by the way. Were you thinking of auditioning?" he asked.

"Yes, I think this play will help me become a better person."

"What do you mean?"

"I'm trying not to be homophobic."

Ryan's eyebrows quirked, and he gave me *The Look*.

"I see," he murmured slowly. "How is unhomophobing yourself working out?"

"Not very good, I think."

Parker hasn't forgiven me yet.

"Which role are you auditioning for?"

I pointed to the casting list. "The bush."

"The bush," he repeated.

"What about you?"

"Hm? Oh, I'm auditioning for the main role," he said, signing his name beside the Romeo casting box. It had the most signatures. He handed me his pen, and I thanked him, carefully writing my name beside the bush casting box.

"I hope you get to be the bush," he said with a smile. What nice dimples.

"Thank you. No one else auditioned for the role, so hopefully, I'll get it."

"Have you thought about auditioning for any of the roles with lines?" he asked, his blue eyes twinkling with something I couldn't quite put my finger on. Probably because I couldn't literally put my finger in his eye, or he'd cry or go blind. Metaphors can be scary sometimes.

"I suppose I could audition for the tree, but trees don't talk either."

Why did I audition for the bush and not the tree? Was I discriminating against plants? I might have to work on that too...

"How about Clark?" he asked, tapping the box below Romeo, snapping me out of my thoughts. Wasn't Clark the love interest of Romeo?

"Many people are auditioning for Clark."

"You'd be another candidate amongst others, perhaps more exceptional than the rest."

"I'm bad with my words."

"You seem fine right now."

"That's because I'm talking with you."

He raised a brow, a smile teasing the corner of his mouth.

"During these past few seconds in which we've exchanged a few words, I believe that a form of trust has built between us." I raised my hand and pinched the air to show him. "This little."

Ryan bit his lower lip, and turned his face away, trying not to laugh. He failed. "You're way too cute."

"Oh." I understood why people looked so awkward when I complimented them. I felt my cheeks grow hot. "Thank you."

His laughter faded, and he held my gaze with those beautiful blue eyes.

"Be my Clark," he gently suggested, and before I could refuse, he added, "I'd be more than happy to help you with your lines."

"I'm sorry, but I don't think I fit the role. I'm sure you'll find a better Clark."

Ryan looked disappointed, but he didn't insist any further. "And I'm sure you'll make a wonderful bush."

"Thank you!"

"I have to go now, my class is starting soon. I guess I'll see you at the auditions?"

"Yes, you probably will."

"Great." Ryan gave me another one of his wonderful smiles before leaving.

"Ryan, you forgot your pen!" I called, realizing that I was still holding it. He looked over his shoulder, and my heart fluttered when his powerful blue eyes met my gaze.

"Keep it." He grinned. "It'll give me another excuse to see you."

Chapter 19: Audition Day

It was audition day.

Back in high school, I had never joined any clubs. I was never good at participating in activities that required social interactions. I'd always say or do something that would cause others to give me *The Look,* and I assumed my presence bothered them, so I thought it was best if I stayed alone. I never thought I'd audition for a play in university. The idea wasn't even a possibility until a few days ago.

I walked down the halls but stopped in my tracks when I saw Parker. He was arguing with a girl, or rather, a girl was arguing with him. Parker looked annoyed and bored.

I frowned. Despite living only a staircase away from each other, it felt like I hadn't seen him in forever. He wore a gray hoodie and a denim jacket over black jeans. Parker made simple clothes look good. He had dark patches under his dark eyes—I guess those were also part of his charm.

The girl began tugging on the sleeve of his jacket in a begging manner. Parker pulled away, running his hand through his messy raven hair before running it over his rough jaw.

"I said no." His voice was harsh.

"Come to the auditions. It'd be great if you could show your girlfriend some support," the girl said. "All you have to do is sit in the audience."

"Do I look like someone who gives a shit about a bunch of losers running around in green leotards?"

"We're not elves."

"Yes, at least elves don't exist."

"Parker," the girl whined.

I didn't want to eavesdrop on their conversation, but the only way to the university's theatre was down this hall. I stood there, hoping they'd leave.

"Will you please come with me? It'll be fun."

"To be or not to be, no thank thee."

While the girl continued to beg, holding his hand and giving him cute little pouts, Parker looked like he was one step away from losing his mind.

"Conan!" called a familiar voice, giving away my presence. Right as I was about to look away, Parker's surprised gaze met mine. I looked over my shoulder and saw Ryan running towards me.

"Hello, Ryan," I said, unable to forget the look in Parker's eyes. "How are you?"

"I'm good, thanks. You?"

"My heart hurts."

"Your head?" he asked.

"No, my heart," I rectified.

There was a short pause.

"Does it happen frequently?"

"Yes, but not like this."

"Do you want me to feel it?" he asked, reaching out to put his palm against my chest. Before he could, Parker snatched his wrist away. He marched towards us when Ryan called my name.

"The fuck do you think you're doing?" Parker snarled, pushing Ryan away. "Keep your filthy hands off of Dandelion."

He blinked, glanced at me, then his face hardened.

"I mean Conan, keep your hands off— Oh, just don't touch him."

"Who are you?" Ryan asked.

"I'm Conan's—" Parker paused. He ran a hand through his hair before shifting his gaze to me. His husky voice almost fell to a whisper. When he looked at me, my breath caught in my throat. He stood so close, yet he seemed so far.

"I dunno. What are we?"

He was no longer talking to Ryan but to me.

"Parker!" The girl who tugged on Parker's sleeves broke our gaze.

"Brianna?" Ryan blinked in surprise.

"Hey, Ryan. I see you've met my boyfriend, Parker."

Boyfriend.

The pain in my heart worsened. I wish it would stop.

She motioned towards Parker as if he was a million-dollar prize. Though, I hope she knew money could never amount to Parker's worth. He was priceless.

"Your boyfriend," Ryan echoed, and for some reason, he was looking at me.

"Yes." She giggled shyly. "Ryan, meet Parker. Parker, sweetie, meet Ryan. Oh, but no need to be jealous. Ryan is just a friend I met in the theatre club."

"It's nice to meet you," Ryan mumbled.

"Wish I could say the same," Parker replied dryly.

Brianna quickly cleared her throat. "So, Ryan, are you auditioning for the winter play?"

"Yeah, we were just heading to the theatre room."

"*We*?" Parker said, stabbing Ryan with a glare. If eyes could kill, he'd be dead.

"Conan and I," Ryan said with a smug grin. Parker looked like he wanted to murder him.

"I'm auditioning for the bush," I told him, hoping that the piece of information would brighten Parker's mood. It didn't. His jaw ticked instead.

"That's great! I'm auditioning for Aura, the evil aunt," said Brianna, putting a hand in front of her mouth and faking an evil laugh which made me giggle.

"I was just on my way to the auditions. I've been trying to convince Parker to come with me, but he's being stubborn."

"Speaking of auditions, we should hurry before we're late," suggested Ryan, checking his watch.

"Great, let's go," Parker said. We all turned towards him in surprise.

Brianna frowned. "I thought you said you didn't want to go."

Parker looked at me, and the intense gaze in his eyes struck me.

"I changed my mind."

"Why?"

"To be a supportive boyfriend."

But for some reason, Parker wasn't looking at Brianna. He was still looking at me.

Before Brianna could ask any more questions, he started walking down the hall. Ryan and I shared an equally confused look, but we followed Parker down the corridor.

Parker slowed his pace, squeezing himself beside Ryan and me before pushing him away with his hip. Ryan staggered sideways, but Parker looked straight ahead with a smug grin, as if he were sharing a private joke with himself. I wondered what was so funny.

Chapter 20: Sick

When we walked into the theatre room, I was overwhelmed by the number of students preparing for the auditions. Three older students and an old lady with horn-rimmed glasses were sitting at a long table in front of the stage. They were probably the judges. Without a word, Parker walked to the audience's seat and sat down, sprawling his long legs out and sliding his hands into his jacket pockets.

He looked bored. It hadn't even been a minute since he's been here, and he looked like he wanted to die.

The girls sitting in the audience gasped and whispered when they saw him, and they quickly started fixing their hair and straightening their clothes.

"Hi, Parker," they hummed in perfect harmony. Had they rehearsed?

Parker's dark eyes remained on me, and I felt like they were pulling me in like magnets.

"Yeah, hi," he mumbled, giving them a lazy wave, eyes still on me. It wasn't until Ryan tapped my shoulder that I broke our gaze.

"Will you go through my lines with me?" he asked.

"Yes, of course." The bush didn't have any lines, so I decided to help Ryan with his.

We went to the stage where the other students were practicing. Ryan seemed popular. Girls did doubletakes when he walked past them; the brave ones called his name and waved at him, blushing furiously when he smiled. Even the boys seemed shy and intimidated by his presence. It fascinated me how one person could create so much change by simply existing.

"I didn't know you were friends with Parker," Ryan said.

The ache in my chest returned.

"I don't think we're friends anymore."

"Why not?"

"I said something that upset him."

Ryan pursed his lips, studying the planes of my face, then shrugged. "Well, if he doesn't realize how lucky he is, then that's his loss. You're a good person, Conan. I'm sure whatever you said wasn't that bad."

I squeezed my fingers. I wanted to tell him that what I said wasn't bad—it was *terrible*. But the fear of losing another friend would destroy me, so I kept silent.

"Thank you for your kind words," was all I said.

Ryan looked at me, and I knew what he was thinking. It made me uncomfortable, so I unconsciously took a step back. Ryan blinked, then looked away, running his hand through his hair before letting it fall to his neck. He quickly cleared his voice.

"Right, let's start with page three," he said, handing me an extra script. "The lines you have to read are underlined in red."

I nodded.

"Oh, Romeo, my dear Romeo..."

We went through the scenes and made it to the part where we ran away from the castle soldiers and hid in a cave. He took a step towards me, and my body squirmed. I tried to focus on the lines.

"The guards will kill us once they find us. They'll have us executed."

My voice sounded stiff and unnatural compared to Ryan's. I admired how easily he read his lines and how well he embodied his character.

I sounded like a bush who was trying to be a person.

"There are so many worse things in life than being in love with a man," Ryan insisted. The conviction in his voice fascinated me, and I felt like I was rehearsing with Romeo, not Ryan.

"Name one," I read flatly, but the text said to speak *passionately*.

"Living a lie," he said. "Letting others dictate the way we live."

I looked down at the script, and it said to look away, so I did and stared at my shoes. They were dirty.

"Please, Clark, look at me," he said. Ryan took another step. I quickly raised my gaze, taking a step back to keep a certain distance between us.

"I have spent my life resisting the desire to want you, but I can't bear it any longer."

I didn't know what the following lines were, but I was afraid if I looked away, he'd touch me. So instead, I improvised and shook my head.

I made the wrong move because he took my hands and pulled me closer to him. I lost my balance and pressed one palm against his chest to prevent myself from falling while the other was crushed in his hand. My entire body froze stiff. My stomach curled, my lungs burned, and I felt the entire room was closing in on me.

Breathe, Conan. Breathe.

But the entire world darkened, and I couldn't see anything. All I could feel were hands slipping into my clothes and touching me, groping me in places that made my body cringe. *The Dark Thoughts.* They were back. I tried to remember what Dr. Philip George told me.

It's not real, it's not real, it's not real...

My breath became heavy, and I felt like I was swallowing damp air that clogged my throat. I wanted to pull away from Ryan, but I heard footsteps. Someone approached me from behind, and I was trapped between Ryan and an invisible demon. I couldn't see who was behind me, but I felt cold lips brush over my earlobe, sending shivers down my spine.

"Where do you think you're going?" the man asked.

"Running," I answered.

"Running?" He cackled. *"Why?"*

Because I'm scared.

"You think you own your body?"

I felt tears prick my eyes. I couldn't breathe. I couldn't move. I couldn't see.

"Stop dreaming, Conan. You make me sick," he spat.

And then everything made sense again. The realization hit me.

That's right. I was sick.

The man vanished, and the hands slithered away. Everything became eerily silent, and I stood there like a corpse. The darkness faded away and reality whirled back into place, and I could see Ryan again, but I wanted to see Parker.

"I would die for you," Ryan said. "Let me love you, Clark. Give me your life and I'll give you mine."

My body was trembling, and tears dripped down my chin. Ryan must have thought it was all part of the act, but it wasn't. My lips quivered uncontrollably, and my shoulders shook in fear.

I wanted to run away and hide from the world, but I knew Parker was watching. I had to prove to him that he had misunderstood what I had said. I didn't hate people like him. I hated myself.

"Okay," I choked, more tears welling in my eyes. I didn't know the next lines.

Ryan's eyebrows creased in worry, unsure whether I was truly in pain or simply acting. He reached out to wipe away my tears, but a thunder of applause broke our gaze. The judges stood up and clapped, and so did everyone standing around us.

"Bravo, bravo! That was brilliant!" exclaimed the professor. She quickly climbed onto the stage with a wide grin.

"The passion, the angst, the chemistry, you two have it all!" she said, stars twinkling in her bright eyes. "Ladies and gentlemen, we've found our Romeo and Clark!"

My heart stopped.

"But the bush…"

"Forget the bush, Conan. We got the lead roles!" Ryan exclaimed.

My eyes frantically searched the audience, hoping that the news would at least make Parker happy. If I was lucky, maybe he'd be my friend again. He might even be proud. But my heart smashed like a watermelon when I saw that Parker's seat was empty.

He was gone.

***

When I told Freddie and Zev about my unexpected role as one of the main leads and my unfortunate missed opportunity to play a wonderful bush, they rejoiced with glee.

"Did you hear that? Our Conan is going to be the main lead!" Freddie exclaimed.

"*One* of the main leads," I tried to clarify.

"The *main* lead!" Zev cried, throwing his hands in the air. "Our baby is the MAIN lead!"

My friends seemed more excited by the news than I was. They were over the moon. They stopped every person passing by and told them I got the role of Clark. The strangers, who had no context whatsoever, gave them *The Look*. But Freddie and Zev were too happy to notice. I felt so lucky.

I sometimes felt as if Freddie and Zev were my parents. Of course, Freddie had a boyfriend, and Zev had a girlfriend, and neither of them gave birth to me, but it still felt like there were my proud fathers. The thought of us being a nice, happy family made my heart feel warm and cozy.

They insisted that we celebrate the good news. I agreed because I'd take any reason to spend more time with them. Zev told us he'd come over and make us one of his mother's famous dishes. Considering how great of a cook he was, we knew we were in for a treat. Zev's mother was a cook, so Zev learned how to make delicious dishes when he was young. He said he'd like to make his own cookbook in the future and said he'd gift us one if he ever published it.

We waited until the weekend to celebrate. The three of us went to the groceries and bought the ingredients. Zev wanted to buy the most expensive items, but Freddie reminded him we were on a college student budget. Zev argued and said I deserve only the best. Freddie agreed but said I could have the best *affordable* items. I took pictures of them as they argued, for memories, and because I wanted to show Parker everything we did since he wasn't here with us. I wondered what he was doing. Did he already have dinner?

They couldn't agree on which products to buy, and both turned towards me for an answer. I smiled at them and told them whatever made them happy made me happy, which probably didn't help their case.

They continued to quarrel like an old married couple, but I still smiled. Going to the groceries all together, it felt like we were family. Although, I wish Parker was with us.

We decided to buy affordable food, but Freddie let me pick the desserts. When we arrived at my place, I received a message. I thought it was Parker, but I felt disappointed when I saw it was Ryan.

Ryan and I exchanged numbers after we were announced as Romeo and Clark. It was the first time he had texted me a message.

Ryan: Hi, Conan. It's me, Ryan. I'm really excited to be able to work with you. What an unexpected turn of events, right? You were amazing. You said you weren't good with your words, but I don't believe it. I'm happy we'll get to see each other more. Are you free this Saturday? Maybe we can rehearse together if you aren't doing anything.

"Ooh-la-la, looks like someone has a date," Zev chirped, looking over my shoulder and peeking at my phone.

"Oh, no, Ryan just wants to rehearse together," I said, showing him the text.

Freddie tilted his head to read it as well. "Definitely a date," he confirmed.

Zev suddenly got on his knees, extending his hand to offer Freddie the bundle of broccoli. "Romeo, oh Romeo, will you take my token of love and ride away into the sunset with me?"

Freddie clutched his heart and let out a dramatic gasp. "Oh Clark, I thought you'd never ask!"

He took the broccoli and threw it over his shoulder, and they both pretended to smooch exaggeratedly. I felt a wave of heat rise to my neck.

"Guys," I murmured, and they burst into laughter.

"We're kidding, we're kidding." Zev winked. "Or are we?"

"Do any of you know if Parker is coming?" I asked, hopeful. "I sent him a message, but he hasn't replied."

Freddie and Zev glanced at each other, and their smile slowly faded.

"Sorry, he hasn't answered my text either," Zev replied.

"Oh, it's okay! Parker must be busy," I said, trying to smile. "He has homework and a girlfriend to take care of."

"I heard he broke up with Brianna. His relationships never last very long," Freddie said.

"Oh."

I felt a stinging pain in my chest.

"I'll try sending him another message, just in case. Maybe he'll get hungry and join us."

They nodded but didn't say anything. I went to the bathroom and closed the door behind me. I crouched down and read the messages I sent Parker.

Me: Hello, Parker! How are you? (December 2)

Me: Hello, Parker! I have some good news I'd like to share with you. Can we see each other? (December 3)

Me: Hello, Parker. You must be busy. I'm sorry for bothering you so much. I wanted to tell you that I got the second lead role in the school play. I hope you are doing well. Please take care of yourself and make sure to wear lots of clothes. It's getting cold. (December 4)

Me: Hello, Parker... I hope you're well. Freddie, Zev, and I are having dinner at my house tonight. Would you like to join us? I hope you can. Please let me know. (Today 8:08 a.m.)

Me: Hello, Parker. We're at the groceries! Would you like us to get you something? (Today 6:01 p.m.)

Me: Hello, Parker! Freddie let me choose the dessert. I chose apple pie because I know how much you love apples. I'll make sure to save you a slice. (Today: 6:15 p.m.)

Parker hadn't answered any of my messages. I cried alone in the bathroom, and I returned to the kitchen once I managed to pull myself together. We made dinner and ate, laughing and talking about everything and anything, but something felt missing—or rather, *someone*. After our party, Freddie and Zev went home. I cleaned up the table and put a filter over the last slice of apple pie. I put it in the fridge.

The garbage was full, so I pulled the bag out of the bin and headed downstairs to throw it out. I recycled the plastic and threw the black garbage bag into the trash. I was about to head back when I saw someone walk out of the building. My eyes brightened. It was Parker.

Chapter 21: We See Life in Death

"Parker!" I exclaimed, running after him. He looked over his shoulder and scowled when he saw me. "Good evening."

"Yeah," he replied, his voice rough and sharp.

"How are you?" I asked, trying not to shiver from the cold.

"Great."

I smiled. "I'm glad."

Parker narrowed his eyes at me. I must have said something wrong.

"I sent you a few texts, but you never replied. Oh, but I know you didn't have any bad intentions—"

"I did."

I paused. "What?"

"I did have bad intentions."

"Oh." I squeezed my hands. I didn't know what to say. "But... Why?"

Parker let out a bitter laugh. "You have got to be kidding me. Forget it. I have to go."

He turned to leave, but I quickly stepped forward.

"Wait, I don't understand."

"That's the thing!" he shouted, making me flinch. "You never understand!"

"I'm sorry, I—"

His head hung, and he ran a frustrated hand through his velvet hair.

"That's not what I want to hear," he muttered. A long silence hung over us, and I waited for him to say something. He looked up with his miserable dark eyes, his disheveled hair falling over his beautiful forehead. "Let's stop this."

"Stop what?" I asked.

"Being friends."

My body stiffened.

"You're going to destroy me all over again," he said, and then he laughed, shaking his head. "You terrify me, Conan. You're small, you're frail, you look like you'd fall over if the wind blew against you, but you're absolutely terrifying."

"I didn't mean to scare you."

"But you did. You still do," he added, looking at me with sadness drowning in his dark eyes. "And it hurts so much."

Parker seemed so normal, I sometimes forgot he had his own problems. It wasn't easy for him to get over the death of his ex-boyfriend. It had left him empty and hurt.

"You're going to destroy me all over again."

For someone who pretended to be shallow, there was a great deal of emotion behind every word he spoke. I stood there, trying to understand what I had done wrong and how I'd hurt Parker. I tried my best to show him that I wasn't broken—

I made an effort to seem repaired. Where did everything go wrong?

I decided to be honest. I decided to use the simplest words that hid no ambiguity or confusion.

"I don't understand," I told him quietly.

"Don't you get it, Conan?" he yelled, his harsh voice making me shrink. He looked so profoundly hurt, as if he was going to cry, but then he replaced whatever vulnerability exposed there with a scowl.

"You're all I think about. You're all I *can* think about. I'm worried about you 24/7, wondering how you're doing, if you're eating, whether you're still *fucking breathing*. Do you think that's normal? Do you know how unpredictable you are? I never know what's going on in your head. Who knows when you'll leave? And when you do, where does that leave me?" he asked, his eyes burning with so much life and pain. "I can't go through this again. I can't. I am this close to losing my mind," he rasped, pinching the air. "And I've just finally started getting better, and then you suddenly arrive and start messing with my head, and fuck!"

He took a step back, his jaw tightening.

"I do care about you," I pressed.

"You don't give a damn!" he roared. "If you cared about me, if you really fucking cared, then you wouldn't be hurting me like this. If you cared, even just a bit, you wouldn't be smiling so widely and laughing, you wouldn't have joined that fucking gay play, and you wouldn't have agreed to play the role with Ryan. I'm here drinking and smoking just to forget what it's like to hear your voice, and you're out there having the time of your life."

My eyes widened.

"Is it fun for you? Rubbing it in my face to show how little I mean to you? You're making a fool out of me, and I can't take it anymore."

I stood there, shocked. I realized that Parker misunderstood my intentions. I envied those who could easily communicate their version of reality to others. They had the gift of dodging miscommunication and misunderstandings. Society was defined by a group of people, but in society, there were individuals, and individuals implied the existence of more than one perception of the world. You had to use the proper words so another could understand you. How was I going to tell Parker that he had misinterpreted my intentions without hurting him?

Think, Conan, think. You have a variety of words, you speak the same language, so why can't you use them properly?

"Go home, Conan," he whispered. Parker was about to leave. I could feel him sleeping out of my hands like sand, and I panicked.

Words, words, words. My mind screamed at me to say something, but I was scared. I knew it would be over for good if I made a mistake. I couldn't lose part, so amidst the rise of panic, I blurted, "I like you."

When the words slipped out, I wanted to cry. The syllables burned my throat and left a bitter taste, and regret hit me like a train. At a young age, too young, perhaps, I realized that my feelings and thoughts were the only things that were truly mine. So why? After years of silence, after keeping everything bottled up inside for so long, why was I taking the risk of letting someone hurt me? Being emotionally vulnerable was no better than choosing your misery.

And yet I had a desperate need to be heard.

"I've been trying," I choked, trying to get the words out of my chest. "And I don't understand what I've done wrong. When I said I was homophobic, I didn't mean I hated you. I can't find another word to explain my pain when I'm too close to men. And I'm sorry if this upsets you, but I'm trying to fix myself. That's why I joined the play and agreed to play Clark. I know you won't be my friend until I fix myself, so I'm trying. But I need a little more time, Parker. I'll... I'll get better, I really will, I just..."

I was thinking so much, feeling so much, I couldn't find my words.

You can't even speak properly, Conan. This is why Parker doesn't want you. You're pathetic.

"Conan," Parker murmured, but I took a step back, shaking my head. He was going to tell me he was going to leave. He was going to leave me alone and tell me he didn't want me.

"Can I please have some more time? I'll try harder," I begged him, feeling immense pain and fear. "Parker, please, I'm sorry, it's my fault—"

Parker reached out and pulled me tightly against his chest. As soon as I was in his arms, my panicking thoughts calmed down instantly. The world felt less cold, less cruel, and less lonely.

Yet, I felt repulsed. It took everything in me not to rip myself away from him. I wish I could hug him back, but I knew my body wouldn't allow it. So I stood there, my fists firmly glued to my sides. I knew I'd lose my mind if I moved even an inch.

And that's who you are, Conan. You're sick.

I didn't notice that I was clutching onto Parker's shirt until my knees gave up, pulling the both of us down.

"I write about you in my journal every day, and I tell doctor Philip George about you, and I was really sad when you ignored me, and I was worried when you didn't answer my texts, and... and..." I tried to show him how much I cared about him, but it was getting harder to breathe, and my chest rose and fell unevenly. "I don't hate you, Parker, I promise. I'm not homophobic towards you."

"It's okay, Conan, it's okay," he whispered into my hair.

I pressed my hands against his chest, and he loosened his grip, allowing me to escape his embrace like a frantic fish given another chance to swim back into the deep, dark sea. I sat on the ground, covering my face, embarrassed and ashamed. My body shook as I sobbed, and I tried to calm myself. But what you wanted and what happened were two very different things. I don't know how long I cried, but eventually, the tears stopped. The pain was still lodged in my chest, but at least the tears were gone. I had cried so much I felt nauseous.

"Conan?" I heard Parker call my name softly. I didn't answer, as if I were dead. Maybe it would be better if I were. "Will you let me see your face?" he whispered. "Please?"

I shook my head.

"I want to see you," he murmured gently. After hesitating for a long moment, I lowered my hands.

"There we go," he said, trying to smile. "Can I touch you?"

I nodded once. He reached out and gently wiped away the remaining tears that stained my cheeks.

"I shouldn't have yelled at you like that. I'm sorry."

I stared at the ground.

"Can I ask you something?" Parker asked.

"Okay."

"When you said you liked me, did you mean as a friend?"

"I don't know."

There was a pause, and he said, "Well, I like you too."

"As a friend?"

He shook his head. "Much more."

I blinked.

"Best friends?"

"I like you romantically," he stated, knowing that I wouldn't understand otherwise. "Does that make more sense?"

It did and it didn't.

"Oh." I felt my cheeks flush red. "Yes, I suppose."

Another silence followed.

"Does that mean we have to hold hands and kiss?" I asked, fiddling with the hem of his shirt.

"Do you want to hold hands and kiss?" he asked, his voice low but soft.

"I'll have to think about it."

I waited a moment.

"I thought about it, but I don't think I'm ready."

"Then we won't," he reassured me.

"But what about you?"

"What about me?"

"You like kissing and hugging. You're always doing it with girls," I murmured, shifting uncomfortably.

He scowled. "I'm not that big of a sex addict."

"But you like it," I insisted.

"Yes, but I like *you* more."

"I don't believe you."

He gasped. "Are you calling me a liar?"

My eyes widened. "N-No! That's not what I meant. I'm so—"

Parker burst into laughter, and my chest tightened. He smiled, resting his jaw against his knuckles. "I was kidding, dandelion."

I pressed my lips together, feeling my face flush hot. He reached out and gently brushed his fingers over my hand. I shivered but didn't pull away.

"I'll wait," he promised me.

"What if you're not happy with me?" I asked nervously, wondering if I was digging my own grave.

"I was never happy anyway. I've got nothing to lose."

"But I'm leaving in a year. What will you do when I'm gone?"

The smile on his face vanished, and his eyes hardened.

"I'll find a way to make you stay," he told me firmly. "For you to *want* to stay."

I could see in Parker's eyes that he was scared, perhaps as much as I was, if not more. Whether it was alcohol or starvation, we depended on unhealthy habits to numb our pain. What good would come from two suffering individuals who only saw life in death?

But despite the inevitable pain we'd bring each other, perhaps there was hope. It wasn't a hope in which we would restore ourselves completely. It was a glimmer of light that was too dim to brighten our entire future but bright enough to give us hope. It was a light we saw in no one else but in each other.

***

After that night, Parker and I began dating. We skipped the conventional dating norms and dated in our way. He'd come over to make me food and ensured that I never missed any of my appointments at his dad's clinic while I kept the bottles away from him and asked him to smoke only one packet of cigarettes instead of two.

Eating had gotten easier, and I began enjoying my meals. It wasn't because I enjoyed filling my stomach but because I loved talking and spending time with Parker at the dinner table. He also bought me dinosaur-shaped vitamins, and we'd each take one every morning before heading to university. It became our ritual.

And that's how Parker and I became friends again. Well, more than friends. We were us.

Chapter 22: Normal People

"I think we should take a break," Ryan said, sitting on the stage. He cracked open a bottle of water and handed it to me, but I shook my head. I sat down beside him at a comfortable distance, watching him tilt his head back and drink. His jawline sharpened when he raised his chin, and his Adam's apple bobbed at each gulp.

"You're very handsome," I told him.

Ryan choked on his water, getting his shirt all wet. He turned his head, coughing while hitting his chest.

"Are you okay?" I asked, worried.

"Yeah," he rasped between coughs, wiping his lips with the back of his hand. "I just wasn't ready for you to say that. I never am."

"Oh, I'm sorry."

I needed to be more careful with my compliments. They seemed counter-productive. Ryan and I had been rehearsing in our university's theatre room the entire afternoon. He helped me with my lines and gave me many acting tips, like how to avoid stuttering or what to do with my hands when speaking.

"You're good at this," I told him, dangling my feet over the edge of the stage. "How long have you been acting?"

"Since middle school. I was one of those geeky theatre losers who was into literature and poetry."

"I love literature and poetry!" I exclaimed, and he chuckled.

"Not many people did in middle school. I was bullied a lot for it," he said with a sheepish smile.

"Bullied for having a passion?"

"For having an unpopular passion. That, and I was overweight. It didn't help that I wore thick square glasses. My entire appearance screamed 'hit me.'" He laughed. "Books and plays were my only friends back then."

Ryan's sad past surprised me. We'd only met recently, and in the rare moments we saw each other, there were girls around him, and he seemed to have many friends. Everyone loved and admired him.

Then I reminded myself that you never really knew anyone. You knew fragments of them, the parts they wanted you to see, but there was an entire realm you didn't know and perhaps never would.

"After I graduated, I told myself that I'd start fresh. I ditched the glasses, put in some contact lenses, and started hitting the gym. I went on crazy diets during the summer before my first year of uni. Now, people treat me differently. I'm no longer seen as the geeky nerd who likes acting but as a handsome student with a hot passion for playwriting. But I'm still the same person, glasses or not."

I could hear the sadness in Ryan's voice.

"Sorry, I must be boring you with my lame childhood stories."

"No, I think it's very nice of you to share something about your past. I admire you for that. I wish I could do the same."

"You're the only one in this school who knows." He smiled shyly, his blue eyes twinkling.

"I am?"

"Yeah."

That made me feel special, so I tried to think of something I could share with Ryan.

"I didn't have any friends in high school either. The only person I could call somewhat of a friend was the cafeteria lady from Russia. We didn't speak the same language, but I felt like she understood me better than those who did."

Ryan looked at me in a way I couldn't quite describe.

"It would have been nice if you and I had met in high school. I think we would have been great friends," I said.

"You're special, Conan, you know that? You think you're a bush, but you're actually the main lead."

I wanted to cry because Ryan was so kind.

"Thank you," I murmured.

He smiled, reaching out to tousle my hair. I remained still, trying to relax my muscles. Ryan's hands were big, and he had muscular arms, but I wanted to tell myself that he wasn't going to hurt me. I stared at my lap when his hands gently ran through my hair.

"I'd like to see you more."

"For rehearsal?" I inquired.

"Sure," he answered, lowering his hand. He was sitting close to me now, and our legs almost touched.

"Do you think we could meet outside of university for rehearsal? My place or yours, whichever you prefer."

Ryan must take his passion for acting seriously. He was always determined to find time to rehearse. I didn't want to disappoint him. Besides, I enjoyed spending time with him. He was a good friend.

"Okay, if you tell me when you're free, we can find a time during the weekend to meet," I told him.

His smile widened. "Perfect!"

I was glad that he was happy.

We left the building, and Ryan told me about his English professor when I saw Parker in the parking lot. He was leaning against his motorcycle, smoking, and a girl was with him. It was the same blond woman I saw the first few days I arrived at the apartment building.

Parker never wore colorful clothes. He didn't have bright hair or eyes, but he always stood out. At that moment, although it wasn't the first, I wanted to reach out and touch him.

The girl he was with did it in my stead. She laughed and stole his cigarette, putting it between her lips with a taunting grin. Parker tried to snatch it back, but she dodged and ran away, climbing onto a table with a triumphing smile. He rolled his eyes, but his lips softened into a smile, and I felt my heart race even though he wasn't smiling at me.

Parker sighed. "Alright, you can have it, just come down from there. I'm not going to take responsibility if you slip and crack your head."

He was right to take precautions. It had snowed heavily last night, and the table the girl was standing on was covered in snow. She took a drag from Parker's cigarette, ignoring his warning.

"You're going to hurt me if I come down," she stated.

He scowled in a mocking way. "What is this? Middle school?"

She shrugged. "I doubt anything can ever be PG-13 with you." She cackled, which made me flinch.

"Will you just come down?" Parker mumbled.

"You promise you won't do anything?"

"I promise," he snapped. Despite his annoyance, he gave out his hand.

The girl hesitated at first but took it and hopped off the table. She almost slipped on the patch of ice she landed on, but Parker caught her arm in the nick of time. He glared at her, but she grinned, too giddy and high on life.

"Idiot," he mumbled, looking annoyed without really being annoyed, and she laughed, saying something to him that I couldn't hear. I was too far away.

So that's what it's like to be normal.

"What are you looking at?" Ryan asked, following my gaze and looking at the two, who continued to argue and laugh.

"Oh, it's Parker," he mumbled, his voice falling flat. "He must have found himself another girlfriend."

My chest tightened, and I couldn't find myself to tell him that Parker was with me. It seemed absurd, even to me. Why would someone like Parker want to be with me, anyway?

"Well, I guess they look cute together," Ryan murmured.

I smiled, but it hurt.

"Yes, they do."

Chapter 23: Infinitely Big

I was at home reading a philosophy book about how the world was infinitely big and humans miserably small. Parker texted me, inviting me to his place. I told him I was busy doing homework, which sadly, was a lie. I didn't want to be with Parker right now. After seeing him with someone else, I couldn't help but think how unfit I was for him and people in general. I felt like a puzzle piece that had fallen off the table and crooked, and no matter how hard you tried to push it back in, it just wouldn't fit. So you set it aside, not with the others but not far away from them either.

I tried to return to my book, but the Dark Thoughts kept creeping into my mind, asking me questions I didn't have answers to.

Why was Parker with me in the first place? Parker liked touching people. He liked it when others touched him. He liked intimacy, he liked kissing, he liked *sex*, he liked everything I couldn't give him, so why was he going through the trouble of being with me? Why even bother?

Then I thought to myself, maybe he *was* having sex with other people. Maybe he was seeing people behind my back and that his patience wasn't real patience but a lie.

Perhaps he enjoyed our conversations, which was why he kept me by his side but confided in someone else for physical pleasure.

Yes, that must be it. There was no logical reason to explain Parker wanting to be with me or why he would deprive himself of pleasure.

I quickly shook my head, trying to push away the Dark Thoughts.

I hated how terrible my mind was. The human mind was a terrible, terrible thing. It transgressed morals. It pondered on all the "what ifs" that ventured the possibilities and impossibilities. There were no limits to our imagination, which was both a gift and a curse. Or perhaps it wasn't the human mind that was terrible, but mine.

You're a terrible person, Conan. How could you think so lowly of Parker? He's been so good to you, and what do you do in return? You think badly of him. You're terrible, Conan. Absolutely terrible.

It was now both my Dark Thoughts and myself who scolded me this time.

I couldn't finish my book and crawled into bed. I cried myself to sleep but didn't feel guilty about crying. No one would see me anyway. I was completely, utterly alone.

Everyone needed their safe place to cry. Some people liked crying in the shower, others in the bathroom. My safe place was in my room, in my bed, under the sheets. It was where I could hide from the world and be myself for a few minutes.

I avoided Parker for the next few days, turning down his invitations and finding excuses not to see him. But on

Friday night, my phone rang, and the Dark Thoughts crawled away as soon as it did. They were scared of Parker.

I answered.

"Dandelion?" His voice made me feel better and worse.

"Good evening, Parker."

"I ordered too much pizza. Come up and help me finish it."

"Oh, I'm not hungry."

"I never asked."

He hung up. I frowned and wondered if I should go or not.

I should go. I have to go.

But I couldn't find the strength to pull myself onto my feet and walk the stairs, so for ten minutes, my mind was telling me to move while my legs remained limp. Then I heard a knock on my door, and I knew I didn't have any other choice but to answer it.

"Good evening, Parker."

He was holding a pizza box and brushed past me, setting it on the table without a word. He motioned for me to sit, so I did.

"Eat," he ordered. I could tell he was in a bad mood.

"Oh, thank you, but I'm not hungry," I repeated.

"Why aren't you hungry?"

"Since I was twelve, I stopped feeling hunger," I informed him.

Parker's brows knitted. "Did you have dinner?"

"No."

"You have to eat," he murmured, and I could see how stressed he was. "Will you eat for me, please?"

Please. That was a word Parker rarely used.

When I didn't answer immediately, he let out a quiet sigh. "Alright, what's wrong?"

"What do you mean?"

"You don't eat when something bothers you. You've been doing well these past few weeks, and suddenly your appetite drops again, so what's wrong?"

I hadn't realized how close Parker and I had become since we began dating.

"Conan, we basically live together," he growled impatiently.

"Yes, I suppose," I answered quietly.

"What's the matter?" he tried again, trying to sound patient. "You've been acting strange, and I'm getting worried."

He looked so deeply into my eyes that I dropped my gaze, unable to bear seeing him hurt.

"I don't want to talk about it," I whispered.

I sounded like a spoiled brat, and perhaps I was. Parker treated me the best he could. He'd raise his voice sometimes, but he'd try to calm himself down whenever he did. He made sure I ate, that I was okay, that I wasn't lonely, and he gave me so much love, attention, and time. What did I give him in return? Pain.

Whenever there wasn't anything wrong, I'd find ways to *make* it wrong. Because if you thought about it, there wasn't anything physically or visibly wrong with me. What was I so sad about? I had food, friends, a family, and all these beautiful things, so why couldn't I be happy?

"You never want to talk about it."

"I can't."

"Why not?" He was growing impatient.

"I just can't."

He took a tight breath, then spoke as softly as he could, sounding tired and drained. "You have to talk to me, dandelion."

My heart pounded against my chest. I could feel the words on the tip of my tongue, all I needed was a little more confidence, a little more time, a gentle push, but as my lips parted, the Dark Thoughts stopped me.

That's right. Tell me him everything. Tell him everything that's wrong with you. Tell him why he should leave you. Go on, Conan, ruin your life.

"May I be excused? I'd like to go to bed," I murmured.

Frustration flashed through Parker's dark eyes. "You can't keep everything bottled up forever!" There was something in that shout, a pain behind it, a raw cry, and a desperate plea for help. He was like a cornered soldier desperately throwing out grenades, scared for his life—scared for mine.

When I didn't reply, Parker tilted his head back and ran his hands over his face, shutting his eyes tight. He opened his eyes again and walked towards me. He pointed at the pizza on my plate.

"This," he growled. "This better be gone when I come back."

My eyes stretched open.

"Where are you going?" I asked frantically.

He didn't answer and stormed towards the door.

"When will you be back?" I asked, but he slammed the door behind him so loudly my bones shook. I felt panic rise in my chest.

What if Parker didn't come back? What if he left me for good? You really did it this time, Conan, you pushed Parker to his limit, and now he was never coming back. Good for you. It's what you deserve. It's your fault anyway. It's all your fault. It's always been your fault.

I pinched my arm, trying to focus the pain elsewhere. *Don't cry, don't cry, don't cry...* I bit my lower lip and ran after him, but he was no longer there when I opened the door.

The house suddenly felt very big, and I, very small. I forced myself to eat the pizza. I chewed and chewed, and even if I didn't want to eat, I continued to swallow, thinking that if I did, it would somehow make Parker come back.

Half an hour later, I heard the doorknob turn and saw Parker at the door. I felt like I could finally breathe again.

"Parker," I murmured. "I didn't think you'd come back."

Parker walked towards me and crouched down, reaching for my hand. He smelled of fresh tobacco, and I realized he had gone out for a smoke. He smoked whenever he was stressed.

"You thought I wouldn't come back," he repeated, a crease forming between his beautiful brows. "But I told you I would."

"I know." I nodded, carefully touching his fingers. "I know you did."

"But you thought I wouldn't. Why?"

His fingers laced between mine and gave me a gentle squeeze, as if to tell me I could trust him. I didn't think I would have had the courage to answer if it weren't for that small gesture.

"The Dark Thoughts."

There was a short pause. I normally found comfort in silence, but not in this one.

"Those thoughts you have, are they always there?" he asked slowly.

"Not always. Sometimes. They come and go but never leave."

He nodded, but only once. I could tell he was trying to remain calm, but he looked heartbroken.

"I would never leave without telling you."

"I know." But I didn't.

He put his strong hand on my cheek, holding my gaze.

"Your thoughts can manipulate your perception of me, and your insecurities can make me look like a monster. They'll persuade you and deform reality, and nothing I can do will stop them, so I want you to know, at least know here," he said, letting his hand fall to the left side of my chest where my heart was. "I want you to know that I have no intentions of purposely hurting you. If I decide to leave, then I'll be the one to tell you, not your Dark Thoughts."

The intensity of his voice and gaze overpowered the demonic thoughts running through my mind.

I nodded. "Okay."

He gently squeezed my hand and stood up, but I quickly tightened my grip around two fingers.

"Will you stay tonight?" I asked in a rush. I didn't want him to leave.

He pursed his lips. "Do you still have some of my clothes here?"

"Yes."

"And my toothbrush?"

"Still there," I promised.

"I didn't bring a sleeping bag. We'll share the bed."

I had a sleeping bag tucked under my bed, and Parker knew that too. He was asking me to make an effort for him.

"Okay," I replied with a nod. It would be the first time we'd sleep in the same bed.

"Okay," he repeated quietly, planting a kiss on my forehead, and I felt the tension between us melt away.

Chapter 24: Our Reality

Dear,

Things have been getting better between Parker and me. It was primarily thanks to Parker. For someone impatient and hot-tempered, he made an effort to be more patient around me. He always wanted to try new things, pushing me to step out of my comfort zone without forcing me to do anything I didn't want to.

They're scared of Parker — I know they are. A few days ago, they returned and told me I didn't deserve Parker and that he would get bored with me.

"He's with you because he pities you," they said.

I almost believed them. Almost. I remembered what Parker had told me when he put his hand against my chest, over my little heart, telling me he'd never purposely hurt me. So I did something I rarely did. I told Parker what worried me with words. If I remember correctly, our conversation went something like this (it might not be completely accurate. I may have forgotten a few of his words... I hope that's okay):

"Parker? Do you miss sleeping with other people?"

"I miss having sex, but I don't miss the people."

We were lying in bed, and he was caressing my hair.

"You can sleep with other people if you'd like."

Parker scowled, tipping up my chin so I'd look him in the eyes. "You're okay if I sleep with someone else?" He sounded displeased.

"No, I'd be upset. But—"

"But what?"

"I want you to be happy."

"I am happy," he said. "With you."

My heart did a funny little dance, and there was a weird feeling in my stomach. It differed from when I wanted to puke as if a million little butterflies were tickling my organs.

It made me nervous, but I didn't hate it. Parker wrapped his strong arms around me and kissed my head, then my cheek, and then my neck, leaving small bites and traces that would remind me that he was with me at that very moment.

I like Parker. I really, really like Parker. I'd like to use a stronger word, but I'm scared. I hope I can tell him one day, at least before I leave.

Parker is brushing his teeth right now. I have to finish writing before he sees my journal.

Yours Truly

***

I went from hating being touched to craving Parker's touch. I could never initiate physical touch with him, so I patiently waited until Parker did. He'd kiss me on the forehead every morning after we took our dinosaur-shaped vitamins.

But on Monday, he didn't. I frowned, wondering what I had done wrong.

"So, when's the play?" Zev asked, breaking me out of my thoughts. We were having lunch in the cafeteria.

"In February. Will you and Freddie come see me?"

"I thought you'd never ask." Zev sniffled, wiping away a fake tear. "I'll bring you the biggest bouquet, don't you worry. And Freddie will bring a huge sign with your name written in bold letters, and we'll wave it around and cheer your name."

He tapped my nose, and I giggled.

"Zev, it's a play, not a basketball game," Freddie reminded him.

"You have to think out of the box," Zev retorted, tapping the side of his head with two fingers. Freddie opened his mouth but decided not to say anything.

Zev looked at me and shrugged. "He's just stressed about our seven-page essay on the European Union," he told me, rustling Freddie's hair.

"It counts for 50% of our grade," Freddie moaned.

Freddie always stressed about his exams, but I believed he'd do great no matter what. He was studious, smart, and ambitious.

"And you'll ace it," Zev told him. "You always do."

Freddie's face flared red, and he looked away.

"I think I upset Parker," I told them.

"Conan, I love you, but no," Zev said.

"The day you upset someone is the day Zev stops eating candy," Freddie added.

Zev chuckled. "No lie there. Besides, Parker seemed okay when I saw him this morning. In fact, he seemed better than usual. He's smiling a lot more."

"Yeah, it's kind of creeping me out." Freddie shivered. "He hasn't looked this happy since—" He pressed his lips together.

"Since his ex-boyfriend?" I finished.

Freddie flinched but nodded.

"Parker dated another boy before Conan?" Zev asked. "I thought Conan was the first. I used to think Parker was straight, but I guess that's my fault. Never judge a book by its cover. But does that mean he's bisexual? Pansexual? He's definitely not asexual."

"I've never asked him about his sexuality, but I don't think he cares much about labels."

"Parker is Parker. I think that's what matters." I smiled shyly.

Freddie and Zev looked at me, then grinned.

"Aw, look at these two lovebirds," Zev gushed.

"I'm getting jealous. What did Parker do to deserve such an angel?" Freddie sighed, shaking his head.

I blushed, looking at my broccoli. I remember the first day of university. Parker and I chatted in the halls after I puked on his shoes. I told him I didn't think I was capable of love, and yet... And yet, here I was. I loved my friends. I loved Parker. I loved so many people. It was impossible *not* to love them.

I'd read in books and blogs how some people couldn't love others until they loved themselves, but I didn't think that was true. Humans were creatures of society, not isolation. I believed you could love others first, perhaps even more than yourself.

Whenever I was with my friends, I felt a certain peacefulness. The world felt less big, less dark, less horrible, and suddenly my world—perhaps not *the* world, but mine— was much brighter, more alive, more spectacular than ever before.

"Why do you think Parker's upset?" Zev asked, and I drifted back to reality.

"He didn't kiss me on the forehead," I answered, dangling my feet uncomfortably. Zev and Freddie burst into laughter, and I felt my cheeks turn pink. I couldn't understand the joke.

"Aw, Conan, don't make that face." Zev chuckled. "Parker probably just forgot."

"Oh."

"Don't worry. He often forgets things. His brain functions only when he has a bio test or when he's worried about you."

"How 'bout you do something special for him so he doesn't forget the next time?" Zev suggested.

"Something special?"

"Yeah," he replied encouragingly. "Isn't Parker always cooking for you two? How about you make him breakfast?"

Breakfast. I had never made breakfast for anyone before.

"Do you think it'll make him happy?" I asked, hopeful.

Zev and Freddie shared a look before turning towards me with wide grins.

"He'll be over the moon."

***

When I returned home, Parker and I had dinner. We studied after eating dessert, and when we went to bed, I put my alarm super early. I woke up the next day and tiptoed to the kitchen. I began making breakfast as quietly as I could. I called Zev to ask him for his fluffy pancake recipe. I could tell he was half asleep when he answered and apologized for bothering him, but Zev sent me a picture and even stayed on the phone to guide me through the steps. An hour later, as the sun was rising, I heard Parker get up from the bed. He came out and stopped in surprise.

"Good morning, Parker."

"What's all this?" he asked, blinking at the table full of food and fruits.

"Breakfast."

"What's the occasion?"

"It's a new day!"

Parker looked at me and laughed. Anyone else would have given me *The Look*, but he no longer did. Instead, he said, "Conan being Conan," a phrase he'd often repeat. We sat down and ate. I tried to talk more and told Parker about my friendship with Ryan and how we were making lots of progress on the play, but he didn't like it when I brought Ryan up, so I changed the subject.

After breakfast, we washed up and got ready for class. I brushed my teeth while Parker shaved, and he brushed his teeth while I combed my hair. I went to the kitchen to do the dishes when we finished getting ready. Parker followed me, leaning his waist against the counter. He crossed his arms over his broad chest, and the muscles in his arms bulged. "Alright, what's going on?"

"Many things, each and every second," I told him.

Parker turned off the sink, and the water stopped.

"I can't wash the dishes if there's no water," I said with a frown.

"You can do the dishes after you look at me."

So I turned towards him, looked him in the eyes, and then turned the sink back on. Parker shut it off again. "You're acting strange."

I didn't know how to answer.

"I see," I murmured.

Parker sighed, taking a step closer to me. "You're not gonna talk?"

I remained silent, and Parker sighed again. "Fine," he grumbled, pushing himself off the counter.

Panic rose in my chest as I felt him slipping away.

"You didn't kiss me on the forehead yesterday," I blurted. My cheeks flared red. I sounded sillier aloud than I did in my head.

"You mean like this?" Parker asked, walking towards me. He put his hand behind my neck and pulled me towards him, kissing me on the forehead. His lips were warm, and he smelled like fresh pine and mint instead of tobacco and alcohol. My heart melted into a puddle.

"Maybe," I whispered. Parker laughed, and it was such a beautiful sound. I kept it pocketed deep inside my mind for the dark days.

"I appreciate everything you've done for me, dandelion. Breakfast, the dishes, the effort to talk. But you could have just asked me."

"Oh."

The world seemed so simple.

"Yeah, oh." He laughed, attacking my forehead with a million kisses. I couldn't help but giggle.

"Better?" he asked, smiling. Parker knew how to date. He knew how to make someone blush, and most of all, he knew how to make someone who didn't deserve love *feel* loved.

"I think I changed my mind," I whispered so quietly, I was afraid he wouldn't hear me. But he did. Parker always did.

"On what?"

"I wouldn't like it if you did this with someone else," I said, wondering if I was too greedy.

"Do what with someone else?" He grinned, feigning innocence.

"Kiss them," I murmured.

Parker tipped up my chin so I'd meet his eyes. Freddie was right. They were the brightest pair of black. They drew in the orange rays of the morning sun. The light kissed his high cheekbones and brow. His chiseled jawline looked sharper, but he looked at me so gently and lovingly that I felt I was on cloud nine.

"Then ask me," he ordered softly. "Ask me not to kiss anyone else."

"I can't."

He frowned. "Why not?"

"I don't deserve it," I murmured.

"Why not?"

"Because..." my voice trailed off. I couldn't finish my sentence.

"The Dark Thoughts. I know, baby, I know," he whispered, gently brushing my bangs away from my face. "But do me a favor and tell the Dark Thoughts to fuck off."

I laughed, and so did he. But then Parker's eyes changed, and he almost looked sad. He was quiet for a moment, our gazes still holding each other.

"What are you thinking about?" I asked.

"You," he whispered, pressing his forehead against mine. "I'm always thinking about you, Dandelion."

I felt roses blossom against my cheeks.

"You're always giving, but you never ask for anything. You don't make requests, you don't demand, and you take nothing for yourself. It's okay to *want*, Conan, especially you, who is constantly doing good to the world. So ask me, tell me, order me not to kiss anyone."

My heart thumped rapidly against my chest. I took in a tight breath and mustered up some courage.

"Parker, would it be okay if you didn't kiss anyone else? Please?"

"I would be more than happy to kiss no one else but you. Any other requests?"

I took a moment to think.

"Can you kiss me on the lips today?"

Parker looked at me in surprise. Before I could take back my words, he pulled me closer against him.

"That can definitely be arranged," he replied, his voice husky. His face lowered to my eye level, and I suddenly felt shy to meet his gaze. "Have you ever kissed anyone?"

"No, but someone has kissed me."

His jaw tightened.

"Did you enjoy it?"

I shook my head.

"Then it doesn't count," he said firmly.

"It doesn't?"

"Nope. Not according to my dictionary."

"You have a dictionary? Can I read it one day?"

"The point is, I'd like you to consider me as your first kiss."

It was impossible to change established facts. As a biology major, Parker knew that too. The past was in the past, but that didn't mean it didn't happen. But perhaps reality didn't have to be the way we perceived it. Perhaps reality was what we made it, just like life. We all needed a little fiction in life, or what boring lives we'd live!

"I'd like that too," I whispered.

Parker leaned forward and pressed his lips against mine. It felt like an electric shock, and I jerked my head back with frightened eyes. Parker said nothing. He didn't react. He didn't scowl. He didn't give me *The Look*. He simply waited for me to decide what would happen next. His hands were around my waist, but they were loose enough so I could slip away if I wanted to.

I could feel the Dark Thoughts crawling into my mind. I could feel my past pulling me away from Parker. I could feel the memories that made me sick. But then I shook my head.

We'll create our own reality.

I pressed my weight on the tip of my toes and kissed Parker. *I* kissed him. I could feel a smile grow against my lips as our kiss deepened. His arms pulled me closer, and his hands scaled up my back, sending tingles down my spine. He leaned away only an inch.

"Open your mouth, Conan," he whispered against my lips. His husky voice made me feel a way I had never felt before. My lips parted, and I felt his tongue slip into my mouth. My hands got lost in his hair, and I felt a desire bubble inside of me for the first time. I desired him. I *desired* Parker, but the feeling went well past wanting pleasure. It was much stronger. I loved him. I didn't say it, but I did.

Parker's hands slid toward my neck, giving it a gentle squeeze. I gasped, opening my mouth wider. He took the chance to deepen our kiss, his tongue gliding and swirling around mine. His bulge pressed against me, and he kissed my cheek, then my ear and his low, raspy breaths that tickled my skin made my knees buckle.

"Sorry," he rasped, lowering his hand but keeping them around my waist. "Was that too much?"

"No, it's okay," I whispered, my mind feeling fuzzy. Part of me wanted us to venture further. Another part of me wanted to hide.

"You're not ready, are you?"

I shook my head, giving him an honest answer.

Parker nodded once. "We'll wait. I actually think it's better if we do. I have some self-control, but not for everything."

I gulped at his wolfish grin.

"We should get ready. Thank you for breakfast."

I blushed. "It was only pancakes."

He shook his head. "I wasn't talking about the food."

Parker kissed me on the lips before walking away.

Book 2: Darker Parker

Prologue

Dear,

Everything was going so well, but I had forgotten that life was unfair. Life was cruel and owed us nothing. It spared us no guilt.

Perhaps the light I saw in your eyes distracted me from reality. Though I didn't regret a second of that illusion, even if it hurts now, I don't regret it. The only regret I had was not being enough for you, Parker.

You had your own problems, your own traumas, your own demons and struggles, but you always took care of me first. I'm sorry I couldn't do the same. I'm sorry, I'm sorry, I'm sorry.

No matter how hard one tries, fate has our futures written in the stars. Trying to rearrange the comets would be as ridiculous as mankind trying to play God. But if humans were born so powerless, why did the Superior Beings not spare us even an inch of happiness?

Why were we doomed to live miserably if the world was already infinitely large and humans miserably small?

Parker calls me Dandelion. He loves the nickname, and so do I, but the reason behind its roots is a sad one. He told me he was afraid if he looked away for even a second, the wind would take me away and turn me into a million particles beyond his grasp.

Little did he know, little did I know, I would be the one to watch Parker drift away first.

Yours Truly

***

A few months had passed. It was no longer winter, and the sun was shining, but it was strangely cold that day. A chill ran down my spine.

I was alone when my phone rang. When it did, I knew. My throat was painfully dry, and my hands were abnormally clammy. My heart raced and my stomach twisted, and my limbs felt weak. I tried to prepare myself during the few seconds I had, but how does one prepare themselves for a tragedy? You simply couldn't.

I mustered up the courage and answered the phone, bringing it to my ear.

"Hello?" The word burned my throat.

"Conan," blurted the frantic voice. My stomach twisted. "Parker, he—" A gut-wrenching sob followed.

My heart stopped. And I knew, I knew, I *knew*.

Author's Note

Dear,

Thank you to everyone who followed Conan and Parker's story. But the adventure doesn't end here! The second book is also available as a paperback. The sequel is called "Darker Parker." Prepare yourselves for a rollercoaster of emotions!

Before you close this book, please make sure to rate and review Conan the Dandelion on Amazon! It would mean the world. I'll see you in book 2!

Yours truly,
I.J Hidee

Made in the USA
Las Vegas, NV
25 October 2024